POWER BUDDIES

First Edition

Published by The Nazca Plains Corporation
Las Vegas, Nevada
2008

ISBN: 978-1-934625-77-4

Published by

The Nazca Plains Corporation ®
4640 Paradise Rd, Suite 141
Las Vegas NV 89109-8000

PUBLISHER'S NOTE
Power Buddies is a work of fiction created wholly by *Lew Bull's* imagination. All characters are fictional and any resemblance to any persons living or deceased is purely by accident. No portion of this book reflects any real person or events.

Cover, Fleshblack
Art Director, Blake Stephens

DEDICATION

For Tony.
Without his care and encouragement
this book could never have been written.

POWER BUDDIES

First Edition

Lew Bull

TABLE OF CONTENTS

PROLOGUE

The stillness of the cool night over Manchester was suddenly shattered by the breaking of glass and its tinkling sound as it hit the concrete floor of the remote factory. The darkened figures crept stealthily through the now opened window and into the building. There was no sound of an alarm, nor any sign of a security guard as the hooded figures crept quietly through the warehouse-shaped main building. No one spoke; only signals were communicated.

A particular storeroom was reached and there was the prize. The figures stopped and stared at what they had come to find. Once again a signal was given and the figures began packing their prize into waiting bags.

Almost immediately, a siren began screaming and lights were switched on, illuminating not only the outer area of the building, but also its interior. The stuttering sound of gunfire reverberated around the building as bullets began to whiz through the air. The figures were under attack but they were retaliating. The sounds of shouting, breaking glass and gunfire filled the building, until after about ten minutes, all remained still.

Chapter 1
CITY GYM

The clang of dumbbells and weights competed with the grunting and groaning of weightlifters and bodybuilders as they went through the motions of their training, creating a harmonious counterpoint. The air within City Gym hung heavy with the pervasive scents of oils, sweat, deodorant and manliness. Music blared over the speakers as the aerobic classes got underway and people communicated loudly with one another. In fact, the entire area was a cacophony of sounds, senses and testosterone.

The day had been long and it was now 6.30 p.m when the after-workers were now getting rid of the day's stresses through various forms of exercise. The sun was still shining outside, something that hadn't happened much this summer, but it was on its journey to below the horizon, and would, within the next two to three hours, have sunk and turned day into night. In fact, it had been one of those glorious dry British summer days, as opposed to one of those notorious wet summer days. The warmth outside the gym as the sun set was comparable to the warmth that was being generated within the confines of the walls of the gym.

Generally, it was those people who wanted to be 'seen' who attended the gym in the afternoon and early evening, and not the hardened competitive bodybuilders, who had spent the better part of the day exercising, so it almost became a fashion show in the evening – not that one could call the scanty clothing that some of the members were wearing, fashion. However, it was both types of crowds that interested Mike. He found the 'in' crowd who frequented the gym in the late afternoons and evenings interesting in the sense that although their bodies were honed and they were usually younger than the day customers, they were more concerned about their personal appearances as perceived through the eyes of others; this gave them a sense of power. Those in the mornings and early afternoons were there to enhance their physical bulkiness and were not concerned about how others perceived them, yet their achievements gave them a sense of self- power. Mike admired the beauty of the evening crowd and the manliness of the day crowd.

As darkness approached, people rounded off their exercises and training and headed for the showers to freshen up and head for home or the bars. The constant beat of the music continued to blare over the speakers, even though the aerobics classes had long concluded, while the chatter of the people continued to attempt to drown its beat. Slowly the gym began to empty of people and by 9.00 p.m. there were probably only seven or eight people left, and these were predominantly the staff members of the gym.

Mike Schwantz was a personal trainer in the gym as well as fulfilling the role of assistant manager, and had been employed there for the past five years. He had seen many members come and go and many people, including celebrities, had been through his hands as a trainer. He was twenty-six years old, six foot three inches tall with dark brown hair, blue eyes and a body that he could be proud to show and which attracted attention, yet his physique was not that of a competitive bodybuilder. In fact, with his good looks, friendly, open, smiling face, finely honed body and charming personality, he was able to attract anyone, male or female. However, it tended to be the males more than the females on whom he focused his attention. His easy-going, friendly persona was liked by all who came into contact with him, and as far as his attitude to work went, he was dedicated and reliable. Under the skin of this muscular young man, lurked a sensitive, caring person, waiting to find Mr. Right with whom to have a meaningful relationship and share his life. However, he was well aware of certain emotions which also lurked within him waiting to satisfy his desires. At this moment in time, Mike was very much unattached and was enjoying life; not necessarily to the full, but he was happy, thanks primarily to the people whom he met at the gym.

Mike had finished his last client's session and was tidying up the gym and preparing to go home for the night, when Steven Bass, the manager, called and asked him if he would mind locking up for him. Mike, without hesitation, answered that he would gladly do so. This indicated the type of person that Mike was – willing and obliging. However, Mike had left home that morning and accidentally closed the latch and locked his house keys inside, so he asked Steven whether he still had the spare house key that Mike had given him to keep in the office in case of an emergency such as this. Steven gave Mike the key before he left and jokingly told him not to lock that one inside and to return it to the gym for safe keeping the following day.

Steven Bass was not what one might expect a gym manager to look like, in other words, muscular; in fact he was particularly ordinary. He didn't seem to fit into the stereotypical bodybuilding mode; instead he was gawky and gangly, but obviously had money to invest in a business, but why he chose the gym business was not known. He was very plain-looking, to the extent that he didn't even seem to fit in with the gym 'in' crowd that flocked to the gym every afternoon and evening either in build or in dress. He looked the type of person who'd led a sedentary life in whatever work he'd been engaged in, prior to coming to manage City Gym.

Steven had only recently been appointed manager, and was not entirely popular with many of the staff or clients because of his brusque manner in dealing with them. He seldom had a civil word to say to anyone and tended to be autocratic in his managerial approach and treated most people with disdain. If one were to sum up Steven Bass, one might conclude that he was a man with a chip on his shoulder, except to some, it was more like an entire tree on his shoulder. He was in his late thirties, married, so he said, yet was a flirt and was always eyeing the young women who came to the gym; however, most seemed to have learned, by word of mouth, to avoid his advances. Other than that, no one really knew much about him. No one had seen or met his wife, nor did he speak about her to staff members, so one wasn't entirely sure if he was married. The only thing that the staff knew about him was that he had never managed a gym before and so it meant that some of his decision-making left much to be desired.

Mike tolerated the man and respected the position that Steven held, but not necessarily the man who held that position. He fully understood that Steven was the boss and so Mike did as he was asked, but Mike never voluntarily offered to do things for Steven; on the other hand, he was only too willing to help some of his buddies or colleagues. Mike prided himself in generally being able to read people's characters and could often sense if someone was trying to use him for their own ulterior motives, a feature which Steven often used.

On packing up his belongings, Steven immediately left the building to go home for the night and Mike started to switch off the lights in an effort to encourage the last few people to leave. He tidied up the weights area, switched off the music and then made his way towards the men's change rooms to see if there were still people getting changed and if so, to hurry them up so that he too could go home.

"Anybody here?" he shouted on entering the change rooms. No one answered.

He wandered between the lockers, picking up the occasional damp towel and putting it in the laundry basket while he made his way towards the shower area. Although he could not hear any water running, he went into the shower area to check that everything was turned off and tidy up.

The shower area consisted of a number of small tiled shower cubicles, each large enough to take two people and one large open-plan shower area, which had eight shower nozzles. As he walked around the shower cubicles, the remaining smells of soap, deodorant and manliness mixed to create a heady, sweet scent.

From one of the shower cubicles he heard a sound much like someone drying himself with a towel. He could hear the flap of the towel, so he headed towards the area from where the sound was coming. He arrived at a shower cubicle and there stood a naked, tall, muscular, blonde guy of about thirty-years of age, slowly rubbing his towel across his shoulders. Mike looked at the man's face, which was rugged and weather-beaten, but not in any way unattractive and noticed that he had soft blue eyes which seemed to burn into one's being, and a scar above the left eye. He didn't recognize the man who continued to dry himself, without taking much cognizance of Mike or acknowledging him.

"Excuse me, sir. Are you nearly ready to leave as we'd like to lock up!" said Mike in his usual cheery voice.

The man never answered, but continued to dry himself, his gaze now on Mike, his eyes penetrating deep into Mike's. Mike met the man's gaze and saw the softness in those eyes that belied the man's rugged appearance and wondered who he was.

Mike had seen many naked men in the showers before, but looking at this one somehow seemed all the more pleasing and interesting to him. Mike's eyes left the man's face and wandered down over the heavy biceps that were being flexed with each movement of the towel and noticed a tattooed eagle on the man's right arm. He also noticed the man's hands as being large with long fingers, but they didn't resemble a workman's hands. However, that was not to say that they had not done their share of work. He was used to seeing muscular men, but there was a corporeal, animalistic, sexuality that exuded from this man that filled Mike with a sense of pleasure.

Mike noticed the man's pectoral muscles were like two swollen mounds each topped with a large, brown protruding nipple that just begged to be manhandled. His broad, tanned shoulders tapered down to a slim waist with washboard abdominals and his legs were like the trunks of Colossus, long and well-developed. Mike's gaze continued down the heaving, buffed, hairless chest with the swollen nipples, to the flat stomach and on to the gentle swinging of an enormous cock with a massive bulbous head, framed by two pendulous balls. Although Mike had noticed the man's muscular legs, it was in the area of the groin that his eyes now remained focused. Even though the man's balls hung heavily, his cock hung even further down, extending past his balls.

'There must be some truth in the saying that the length of a man's penis can be estimated by the length of his fingers', thought Mike, looking at the long digits and the long appendage.

Throughout Mike's 'inspection' of the man, the guy had never taken his eyes off Mike, nor had he stopped drying himself.

Finally the man spoke.

"Are you in such a hurry to close?" drawled the man with no distinct accent and without any facial reaction, other than his constant stare into Mike's eyes.

Mike wasn't paying much attention to what the man had said; his attention was still focused around the groin area, where the man had now spread his legs apart and was sliding the towel between his legs to dry them. The towel moved slowly and seductively back and forth scooping up his large balls and cock as the towel was pulled forward and then dragging them towards his ass as he pulled the towel back through his legs. Throughout this slow action, both men stared at each other, the man into Mike's face and Mike at the central action that was taking place in the groin area.

A warm feeling began to arise between Mike's legs and he could feel his cock beginning to take on a life of its own within the Lycra shorts he was wearing.

Eventually, still staring into Mike's face, the man spoke again.

"Are you sure that you want to close so soon?" drawled the voice.

The man had obviously seen Mike's physical reaction because Mike could see that a similar swelling was happening to the man. As the towel continued its slow, seductive movement back and forth, so the thickness and length of the man's cock grew until his cock had become fully erect, flat against his hairless stomach. The man stopped drying himself and dropped the towel to the floor of the shower cubicle. He stood tall, legs akimbo, and ran his right hand across his left pectoral, stopping only to flick a finger over the tip of his nipple. Mike watched, fascinated. A slight smile appeared on the man's face.

Mike felt an urge to move into the shower cubicle and touch the man, something he'd never normally do to anyone in the gym for fear of others seeing the physical connection between him and the other person, but as most of the clients had left, he felt a little more confident now; so he stepped into the cubicle with the guy and as he did so, realized for the first time that the floor of the cubicle was dry. Mike looked at the dry floor and then back into the man's blue eyes. If the guy had showered, why was the floor not wet? Mike quickly pushed this thought out of his head and stretched out a hand to touch the man, but he hesitated.

The man continued to play with his nipples, still supplying Mike with the slightest of smiles. Mike's hands moved closer to the man and soon he brought his hands into contact with the man's chest. He dragged the palm of his hand across the man's nipples and then cupped both pecs. The man never took his eyes off Mike's face. Mike felt a wave of excitement, almost like an electric shock pass through his body as he touched the man. The man allowed Mike to run his fingers over his chest, squeezing each nipple ever so gently as he did so. As Mike's hands caressed the man's nipples, the man's head was thrown back and a deep sigh was heard.

A breath of warm air came deep from the man's lungs and his huge powerful hands then pushed down gently on Mike's shoulders, forcing him onto his knees. Mike's hands followed the contours of the man's body as he lowered himself until he knelt face- to-face with the man's throbbing erection. Mike's own cock was stretching the Lycra material of his shorts as it protruded from his groin. Mike didn't need an invitation to what was expected next. He opened his mouth and engulfed the man's engorged cock …

Everything happened so quickly that the last Mike remembered was a feeling of delirium overcoming him and he felt as though he were going to faint and go into a stupor.

Chapter 2
COMING ROUND

"Mike! Mike! Are you Okay?"

Mike opened his eyes. He was lying on the cold shower cubicle floor with Steven Bass standing over him. Mike half raised himself and looked down at his Lycra shorts and noticed there was a wet patch in the front.

"What happened? What are you doing on the floor?"

"I don't actually remember," stammered Mike, sitting up on the cold floor and resting his back against the cubicle wall. "Where's the guy that was here?" asked Mike, a little bewildered.

"What guy?" asked Steven. "I was half way home when I remembered that I'd forgotten something in the office, so I turned back. When I came into the gym, I noticed some of the lights were still shining so I came looking for you and found you lying on the floor here; but what guy are you talking about?"

Mike shook his head, as though trying to wake himself from some dream-like state. "I don't know who he was. I've never seen him here before," replied Mike.

"What did he look like?"

Mike thought about it for a moment and then said, "He was tall, extremely well built, a definite bodybuilder – about thirty." He hesitated for a moment and then added, "Oh and I remember seeing a tattoo of an eagle on his right arm and a scar above his left eye."

"Did he attack you?"

"No," answered Mike. "On the contrary, he wasn't threatening at all. The last I remember was he was standing in the shower cubicle and I had told him that we were closing up for the night…"

Mike hesitated, as he didn't want to tell Steven what had actually happened between himself and the man in the shower, although he couldn't entirely remember himself. In any case, as there was no guy around now, how would Steven believe him? He slowly picked himself up from the cold floor and ran his hand over his wet crotch, which was still slightly engorged.

Steven noticed this and asked with a wry smile, "What happened there?"

Mike could feel his embarrassment and didn't know how to answer.

"Are you sure that you didn't fall asleep in the shower and have a wet dream?" was the snide comment from Steven.

Mike glared at Steven. He was used to these types of comments from his boss, so he turned on his heels choosing to ignore it and, picking up a towel to dry his wet Lycra shorts, walked out of the shower area and headed towards the main part of the gym to continue switching off the lights and locking up for the night. The last Mike heard from Steven was the front door to the gym slamming shut as Steven once again headed home.

When Mike had locked up and gone to his car, he sat there for some time pondering on the evening's events, wondering where this man came from and who he was.

When he got back to his apartment, he poured himself a drink and sat in the darkness of his simply furnished lounge thinking about the man. He couldn't get him out of his mind no matter how hard he tried. He kept seeing the rugged face and the muscular torso and the long, pendulous cock, but a question kept surfacing: who was he? He'd never seen him at the gym before and he was familiar with all the clients, even the very new members. However, Mike had to admit that this guy was different. There was something absorbing about this man who was rugged, sexy and good looking, in a rough way, as well as being mysterious.

Chapter 3
BRETT'S SESSION

The following morning, after a sleepless night, when Mike went into the gym to work, he described the man he had confronted in the showers to a number of his fellow trainers whom he could trust, without divulging too much of what had happened in the shower cubicle, and asked if they knew who the man might be, but to no avail; no one knew who Mike was talking about, nor had any of them seen the guy. In fact, there were times when he began to doubt his own judgment and wondered whether this was all a figment of his imagination. However, as the day progressed, he forgot about the previous day's events and set his mind on his work.

At approximately three in the afternoon, just before the fashion brigade arrived, Brett Hannant, a policeman friend of Mike's, arrived for his training session. Although Mike and Brett had not gone to the same school, they had grown up in the same town and had been friends for many years. They had enjoyed playing sport against each other and were both quite competitive, and had also socialized together as they had been growing up. Both had gone through similar teenage stages of having girlfriends, but at the moment, Mike was single. He had introduced Brett to his current girlfriend, and the two men liked each other a great deal.

Brett was a little shorter in height and was not as bulky as Mike, yet he too had a finely tuned body. He had played a great deal of sport when he was much younger so his body had had an early development. What was happening now, at a later age, was that Brett was refining and toning his natural physique, almost in competition to Mike.

They chatted about work and what they'd been doing lately and the training session that Mike had prepared for Brett for the afternoon, but Mike never mentioned anything pertaining to his previous evening's experience.

Brett went into the change room and changed into his gym clothes and the training session got underway. However, Brett noticed that during the session, Mike didn't seem to have his mind on the activities at hand and asked, "What's troubling you, buddy?"

"What do you mean?"

"Well, it just seems to me that your mind is elsewhere and certainly not here. Are you in love?"

"What?" exclaimed Mike. "No, it's nothing, really. It's just been one of those days I suppose," said Mike, trying to laugh off his friend's concern.

"Spill the beans, buddy. I know you too well. There is something troubling you and maybe I can help."

Mike wasn't sure how to explain the previous day's events to Brett, not knowing how he'd take it. After a little hesitation and some cajoling from Brett, Mike opened up.

"Something happened after work yesterday that I cannot explain," said Mike.

"Cannot explain or don't want to?"

"Cannot."

"Why, what happened?"

Mike tried his best to explain the events to Brett without giving any details of a sexual nature to him.

"I just felt faint," said Mike, "and that's it."

Although Mike put it down to a simple faint, Brett wasn't accepting Mike's version.

"Listen buddy, I've known you long enough and you seem to forget that I'm a cop so I know when I'm being fed misinformation. Now, what really happened?"

"It's exactly as I told you," remonstrated Mike. "I came round with Steven standing over me and I was lying on the floor of a shower cubicle."

"Did this guy that you speak of, hit you?"

"No."

"Did you slip on the floor, perhaps?"

"No, I would have known. In any case, the floor was dry," replied Mike, somewhat irritated. "Listen, don't worry about it."

"What do you mean the floor was dry? Didn't you say the guy was in the shower?"

"Yes, but there was no water on the floor, so I don't know whether he'd showered in another cubicle and then moved into the one I found him in, in order to dry himself, or whether he hadn't showered at all."

"You don't normally shower in one and dry yourself in another," was Brett's immediate response. "What did this guy look like?" asked Brett.

"Well-built, like a brick shit-house, a bit weather-beaten and rugged… oh, and a tattoo on his right arm and a scar above his left eye."

"That sounds like it could be anybody," laughed Brett.

"Sure, but I've never seen him here before; that's the strange part. I know everyone here, even the new guys. It's part of my job to know everyone that comes here."

"Maybe he started yesterday and you hadn't met him yet."

"No, I get to meet all the new members the minute that they join; it's one of my duties. There was just something strange about this guy that I can't explain."

Mike went into a deep thought as his mind re-visited the previous day's event. The whole scene flashed before him once again and it troubled him that he didn't know who this person was yet he had to admit to himself that he found him attractive.

"Well, keep your eyes open for the guy and if you see him ask him who he is and what happened," said Brett, bringing Mike back to the immediate world and starting to do his bench-press exercises.

Brett lay on his back on the bench while Mike helped to lift the metal bar with the weights for him. Brett took the strain and lifted the weights, his arm muscles straining as he did so.

Mike was glad that he had not mentioned any of the sexual activities with the stranger to Brett, but as he thought about the man in the shower, he could feel the initial tinges of a hard-on forming in his Lycra shorts.

As Brett lay on the bench, facing upwards lifting the weights bar, he couldn't but help noticing the bulge forming in Mike's shorts above his face. His eyes focused on this view while he tried desperately to concentrate on the task at hand of lifting his weights, but without much success. As he surveyed the view above him, he could feel his own cock flex inside his sweat pants. He had admired Mike's physique, but this physical reaction seemed unnatural to him. He and Mike had been friends for some time, but nothing sexual had ever arisen between them. In fact Brett considered his friend to be straight and Brett had a girlfriend, but somehow, looking up at Mike standing above him was now doing something to him that he couldn't explain.

On one of his lifts of the weights, Brett's hand brushed across Mike's crotch as he lifted the bar, but Mike had not withdrawn or reacted. He felt a slight hardness in Mike's shorts, but Mike said nothing. Brett continued to raise and lower the bar with the weights on, but could feel his cock straining against the elastic of his sweat pants and he was sure that Mike could see the protruding bulge against the flat stomach, but still Mike never reacted.

Brett placed the bar back in its rack, with Mike's assistance, and sat up, wiping some of the sweat from his brow.

"I think I've had enough for today. I think I'll cut short the session and take a cold shower and cool off," he said, rising from the bench and grabbing his towel.

"But you've done nothing yet," said Mike, a little surprised at Brett cutting short his training session. "If you feel tired of the workout, then that's fine for today. We can always make up the programme tomorrow."

Brett ignored Mike's last statement and made his way to the showers while Mike went to the reception desk with his hard-on subsiding. In his mind, Brett had wondered whether Mike might perhaps follow him into the showers, but it didn't happen. Although, if Mike had done so, Brett wasn't sure what he would have done.

When Brett entered the shower area, he stripped off and, wrapping his towel around his waist and subsiding erection, headed for a shower cubicle. He passed the communal shower where three men were showering and chatting quietly to one another as the water cascaded over them, but decided not to join them as his hard-on had not fully subsided and he was not about to divulge his erection to these men. As he neared the cubicles, he saw a foot protruding from one of the cubicles. When he reached the cubicle he saw the naked body of a young man lying on the wet shower floor, water still pouring from the shower nozzle and a trickle of blood oozing from a gash on the man's head. Brett turned off the water, undid his towel and, lifting the young man's head, placed the towel under it. The young man groaned and his eyes fluttered open.

"What happened to you?"

"Ugh! My head hurts."

"Looks like you've cut it, but not too badly," replied Brett. "What happened?"

The young man merely groaned and tried to take in his surroundings.

"Just lie there and I'll get help for you."

Brett got up, found another towel to wrap around himself and ran to the reception desk where Mike was standing, to seek assistance and get medical aid. Mike was a little surprised to see Brett dressed as he was, in the reception area.

"Mike, I'm sorry to bother you, but I think you'd better come to the showers, some guy's had an accident."

Mike grabbed a first-aid box and both men then ran to the shower area, where they found the young man still lying on the shower floor.

When Mike recognized the guy on the floor, he knelt down beside him and started to dab at the cut with a dry towel.

"Alan, what happened?"

"The last thing I remember was standing under the shower and then I blacked out."

"Did you feel dizzy?" asked Brett.

"No, that's the funny thing. There was no warning. I just felt a heady rush and then feeling delirious. Then I came around with you kneeling over me," said Alan, pointing to Brett.

Mike realized that neither Alan nor Brett knew each other. "I'm sorry, Alan this guy who found you is a friend of mine, Inspector Brett Hannant; Brett this is Alan."

With introductions over, Mike looked at the gash on Alan's head and saw that it was just a tiny tear in the skin and nothing that needed stitches. He cleaned the cut with disinfectant and placed a sticking plaster over it.

"Thanks for finding me," said Alan trying to stand, with the help of Mike and Brett, and get his footing on the wet floor.

"Was there anyone else in the showers at the time you blacked out?" asked Brett.

"Yes, actually there was a very big guy here, but I don't know who he was."

"What did he look like?" asked Mike.

"He was very big, rugged, didn't say anything and had blonde hair," answered Alan.

"Anything else?" asked Brett.

"Hmm, not that I can remember." He paused a while as he held his head and tried to remember. "No wait a minute. He had a scar over his left eye."

Brett and Mike looked at each other, but never said a word. The look was all-knowing. Mike continued to check Alan's head for any other cuts or bumps.

"Listen, I'm finishing work early today," said Mike. "Would you like me to give you a lift home, Alan?"

"I'm sure that I'll be fine to get the train home. Thanks all the same."

"Forget it, you're in no state to go home alone. You've had a bad experience and there could be delayed shock. I'll drop you off at your place, so get dressed and wait for me," replied Mike.

They helped Alan out of the shower and he and Brett went off to the change rooms to dress while Mike walked back to the reception area. Brett finished dressing first and went to the reception area to speak to Mike before leaving.

"I'm going to see if I can get anything else out of him about that incident in the shower," said Mike. "It sounds as though it's the same guy that I encountered. But you know what I find strange is that I've never seen this scarred-faced guy anywhere in the gym other than in the shower area."

"Listen, I'm going back to the office," said Brett.

"But it's so late!"

"Not to worry, I'll see if I can find anything on the computer. Maybe it's someone who has a record and I'll be able to get some info. If I find anything I'll give you a call, otherwise I'll see you here tomorrow."

Chapter 4
ALAN'S HOME

Alan's apartment was modern and immaculate. For a nineteen-year old junior journalist for a newspaper, it seemed a little odd to Mike that such a young man could afford such exquisite furnishings and possess such good taste in décor. Although it was not a large apartment, it remained cozy and intimate, yet not stifling. Mike had taken Alan home after his 'accident' and Alan had invited Mike to join him for a drink.

Alan threw his kitbag onto a wingback chair while Mike made himself comfortable on the leather couch, which was framed by a huge window overlooking the Thames River.

"This is a beautiful setting, Alan. Stunning views and tasteful furnishings."

"Thanks Mike, but the furnishings are thanks to my Mum. She decided on what she thought was necessary for this place and all I had to do was move in. But listen to me droning on. What can I get you to drink?"

"Beer's fine thanks Alan, if you have!"

Alan made his way to the kitchen.

"Make yourself at home," he shouted from the kitchen. "Have a look around if you like."

Mike rose from the couch and looked out of the window across the river, watching the lights twinkling from the buildings and being reflected on the river and noticed the odd boat float by, and then he had a look around the lounge. The room was tidy and simply but elegantly furnished, yet nothing in it seemed to reflect Alan's character. Although the furnishings were modern, it didn't seem to be the choice of a nineteen-year old gay man. Admittedly he knew the tastes of some gay men and this would have been appropriate to them, but somehow Mike didn't think it fitted Alan. Most nineteen-year olds that Mike knew were usually untidy or living with borrowed furniture. This apartment contained neither. Mike surveyed one of the paintings on the lounge wall and decided that Alan had definitely not chosen it. It reflected a still life painting of a bowl of roses. Although it was beautifully captured, it did not seem to capture the character of Alan. Mike did not see Alan as being a 'rose' type person, but then perhaps he was being judgmental. He could see that Alan's family had money, but he felt that everything reflected the family money and not the young man's individuality. Having surveyed the room, Mike made his way into the kitchen where Alan was busy pouring drinks for them.

"Have you had a look around?" asked Alan, pouring a beer.

"Just the lounge and now the kitchen. I really like this place. The view is magnificent, especially at night."

Mike meant what he had said, but he felt that he would have liked to have seen some of Alan's influence in the home.

"I'll show you the rest of the place."

Alan handed Mike his beer and led the way on a tour of the apartment.

Mike followed Alan, admiring the young man's lean, strong legs that led up to a cute rounded ass encased in a pair of pale blue running shorts.

"This is the bathroom," said Alan, with the wave of an arm, "with a Jacuzzi bath and large shower, big enough for at least three."

Mike took in the beautiful bathroom with its pastel shades and his thoughts went to the Jacuzzi and wondered whether Alan ever shared it with anyone. Alan caught Mike eyeing the Jacuzzi and merely smiled at him, knowingly.

"It does get used," he smiled.

They then went down a short corridor and into the master bedroom.

"This is my haven," said Alan. "When I'm stressed, I simply lie on my bed and watch the boats floating along the river," he said, throwing himself onto the bed.

The room had ceiling-to-floor windows which allowed for beautiful views and plenty of light. The bed was also large enough to hold three or four people comfortably and the room was similar to the lounge in furnishing design.

Mike again admired the color scheme and décor and the view from the window and wondered whether mother had influenced the décor in this room as well. The pale yellow walls seemed to create warmth which Mike felt was indicative of Alan's nature, but the décor consisting of heavy curtaining, a Louis XIV chair and two more still life paintings, was definitely mother. It revealed opulence but Alan was not materialistic in that sense of the word. Yes there was wealth apparent in the apartment, but if Alan had his own way and had unlimited funds, Mike was sure that Alan would have decorated his apartment differently.

He turned to face Alan, still lying on the bed. "This really is a beautiful setting, Alan. You're a very fortunate young man." Although he meant what he'd said, he felt a little disheartened that there was nothing of Alan in the apartment, except the young man himself.

"I suppose I am," said Alan rising from the bed and crossing to the window, "but sometimes it gets a bit lonely you know."

He stood before the window with a distant look in his eyes, staring at the river.

The moment seemed to hang in the air. Mike stood next to Alan and saw their reflections in the window. Mike looked handsome and strong standing next to Alan; not that Alan was bad looking or a weakling, in fact because of his looks he could have anyone he wanted, but Mike felt protective of this young man. He wondered about Alan's statement about being 'lonely' and thought it strange that such an attractive young man should be lonely. Mike had ideas that men would be throwing themselves at Alan's feet to get into his pants.

"Come on, let's go and sit down in the lounge; I want to talk to you a little more," said Mike, breaking the moment and bringing Alan back to reality.

The two made their way back into the lounge where Mike made himself comfortable once more on the leather couch, while Alan sat in an easy chair opposite him.

"How long have you been coming to the gym?" enquired Mike.

"Coming up for six months," replied Alan. "Do you think the hard work has paid off?"

"Absolutely," answered Mike, admiring the young man's body. "I've always admired the way in which you go about taking your training sessions seriously."

"You mean you've been watching me at gym?"

"Well not 'watching' as in spying," replied Mike, feeling as though he'd been caught out, "but watching with interest at your advancement."

"Oh," smiled Alan

"Sure. When I see you I don't see a nineteen-year old like other nineteen-year olds, I see a young man. You seem more mature than other young guys the same age; in fact, and I don't mean this in a derogatory way, you don't look like a nineteen-year old."

"Thanks Mike. I take that as a compliment. I know some people always try to look younger than what they are, but I prefer to look older or more mature-looking. I think that's also why I prefer older people."

While they sat there making small talk, Mike found it difficult to take his eyes off the young man's serene, open face. He sat thinking about Alan's statement about being lonely and wondered why such a decent, good-looking young man didn't have someone in his life.

As they chatted Mike noticed the way in which Alan was sitting, with his long, well-formed legs stretched out in front of him, making the front of his running shorts stretch tightly across his crotch. Mike could see the bulge encased in the blue material and could feel a twinge in his own cock. As they chatted, Alan sat balancing his beer glass on his crotch and Mike noticed that every now and again, Alan seemed to push the glass down on his crotch. Watching this action was making it difficult for Mike to control his own cock's reactions to what he saw. Mike was still wearing his Lycra shorts and realized it was becoming awkward for him to hide his rising erection. He adjusted his position on the couch, but it still didn't seem to help. He certainly found Alan attractive but was Alan merely being a tease and goading him or was there something suggestive about his actions?

He had seen the young man naked in the shower and liked what he'd seen, but was this young man really interested in Mike; a nineteen-year old interested in a twenty-six year old? Most young men of Alan's age were more interested in guys or girls their own age or younger, but rarely older men, although Alan had said that he preferred older people. However, what was age? Merely a state of mind thought Mike.

Mike took a sip of his beer and held the glass on his ever-growing crotch.

"Alan, may I ask you something about the incident today?"

"Sure, fire away!" said the young man, smiling angelically towards Mike.

"I know this might be personal, and if you don't wish to answer, I'll understand."

"Go for it," was the reply.

Mike sat forward, trying to be in closer proximity to Alan. "Firstly, when you went for a shower, were there three guys in the communal shower?"

"What three guys? There was nobody in the shower area except me."

"Brett merely noted that when he went into the shower area there were three guys in the communal shower area."

"I didn't see any other guys there."

"OK. Secondly, were you in the shower with that big guy?" continued Mike.

Alan looked a little embarrassed and tried to avoid the question.

"I'm sorry to ask you this. What I mean is, were you in the shower together, sharing the shower?"

Mike realized Alan's embarrassment and tried to make it easier for the young man, when he continued, "I'm sorry. I know I shouldn't have asked you something personal like that, it's just that a similar thing happened to me."

Alan looked surprised by Mike's statement.

"What do you mean it happened to you?"

Mike took Alan into his confidence and told him what had happened, including some of the sexual details, and that he too had blacked out and Steven had found him on the shower floor. "Tell me what happened in your case," Mike asked in a more empathetic tone.

Alan's voice went soft as he spoke, almost as though he didn't want anyone to hear his story.

"I was in the shower enjoying the coolness of the water when I noticed this big, blonde, guy standing at my shower cubicle entrance staring at me."

"Was he clothed or naked?" Mike asked.

"Naked," replied Alan, a little hesitantly, blushing as he said it.

"And then?"

"He stood there for some time and watched the water running over my body. I must confess that his watching me like that was beginning to worry me. Although I was a little perturbed by his watching me, I actually found him extremely sexy and the fact that he was watching me made it difficult for me to control myself."

Alan paused for a moment as he tried to sort out his thoughts about the event.

"I was beginning … uhm … to get a hard-on," he continued, "so I turned away, hoping that he'd go. I busied myself soaping my chest and arms and then he entered the cubicle and stood behind me under the water. He never spoke at all throughout the whole incident. Somehow I wanted him to touch me, but wasn't sure whether I should let him."

Again Alan hesitated.

"Go on."

"Well, I felt his body was right up against mine. I could feel his cock … rest up against my ass … and felt his breathing as his chest rose and fell against my back. Eventually, I couldn't resist him any more and I had to touch him."

"What did you do?"

"I turned around and faced him, then ran my hands … over his puffed chest, feeling the soft skin covering the hard muscle", said Alan, running his hands over his own chest as he spoke. "By the time I did that, I remember … that both he and I had enormous erections … and our cocks rubbed up against each other's." Alan hesitated as if in deep thought; probably reliving the experience. "The last I remember were his strong arms around me, pulling me closer to him and … his mouth covering mine… then you guys arrived."

When he had finished his description of the events, the two men sat staring silently at each other while Alan ran a hand over his swollen crotch to adjust his penis's position. Mike had to do likewise.

"So he didn't hit you?"

"No, I must have bumped my head on the shower tap when I fell."

"And you don't remember him doing anything else to you?"

"No, but then I wouldn't know because I passed out. You said that a similar thing happened to you. Did it involve the same guy?"

"I think so, or at least it sounds as though it's the same guy."

"Did anything more happen to you than what you told me earlier?" asked Alan.

When Mike heard Alan ask this question, his already erect cock throbbed at the thought of what happened in the shower with him and the strange guy.

Mike searched his memory but hadn't left anything out of the story that he felt he could tell Alan. He noticed that Alan adjusted the position of his hard-on in his running shorts again.

Once Alan had related the evening's events to Mike, they changed the topic of conversation and Alan then said that he was going to take a quick shower and get out of his running gear and that they might go and have something to eat.

Alan rose from his sitting position and headed towards the bathroom.

Mike's eyes followed the young man's sturdy frame as he left the lounge.

"Put some music on if you'd like," shouted Alan from the bathroom.

Mike heard the shower turned on and the splashing of the water onto the floor. He rose from the couch and turned to look out of the window. The glow from the city lights lit up the river and the lounge.

As the water in the shower continued to run, Mike edged closer to the bathroom door. He stood gazing through the open bathroom door at the steaming shower. He could see Alan standing under the water, head thrown back, and water slowly splashing onto his body. Mike watched for a while, then he quietly entered through the bathroom doorway. Alan saw him but didn't react negatively. Instead, he smiled through the shower glass at Mike and winked. Mike accepted the wink as an invitation to join Alan. He stripped off his T-shirt and Lycra shorts and stepped into the shower and felt the warmth of the water and the warmth of Alan's body up against his. Alan admired Mike's well-toned body and had a desire to be held in the confines of his muscular arms, to be smothered with kisses and to be dominated by this older man.

The water streamed down over their entangled bodies as they kissed each other and let their hands roam over each other's body in search of pleasure. Mike placed his arms around Alan's waist and pulled him closer, allowing their rigid cocks to rub up against each other. As their tongues searched within the confines of the other's mouth, so their bodies thrust against each other's and Alan gave himself over to Mike's strength.

When both men had been satisfied, they stepped out of the shower and lovingly dried each other.

Chapter 5
EVENING OUT

Mike and Alan were seated at a table at Alan's local pub, enjoying a drink and each other's company. Although they had known each other only six months and seen each other regularly at the gym, this was the first time that they had gone out together in an evening. Mike found Alan's fresh face and trim body most appealing, something that he was not accustomed to. He did not usually take much notice of younger guys, but to him, Alan had a mysterious appeal that he couldn't explain. He found Alan sexually attractive to the extent that he felt wonderful when he held Alan in his arms, as he'd done in the shower and felt that he was protecting this handsome young man from others. He knew that the young man came from a wealthy background and that he was not your average nineteen-year old teenager, but other than that, he was an enigma.

Mike had never had a lasting relationship with anyone, male or female, simply because he felt that he was always on the lookout for something better. He would go into a relationship with someone and soon find that although he wanted to dominate his partner, there were urges within him that made him hunger to be dominated by someone more powerful than himself and this would lead to a break up between the two parties. However, in his mind, he was not in the process of intentionally making a go of it with Alan, but somehow he was finding himself becoming more attracted to the young man – not only attracted, but also intrigued. Which was taking over, his heart or his head?

He found Alan an extremely attractive person, but again, in Mike's mind, age came into the equation. One half of Mike's subconscious said that he could quite easily have a relationship with Alan – he could care for him, but did Alan want another father figure – a position in which Mike perceived himself, should they have a relationship? The other half of his subconscious was saying, let Alan merely be a good friend and a casual fuck – but that wasn't exactly what Mike wanted. Yes, he was sure that he could enjoy making love to Alan and loving him, but on the other hand did he want only one man in his life? Would he be satiated with one man in his life – in other words, settled in a monogamous relationship? He thought of the man in the shower, whom he had found sexually stimulating and then of Alan and tried to push these thoughts from his mind as it was not as though he had to make a decision there and then in the pub.

Through his conversations with Alan, he had found out that the family's money had been made via the diamond mines of South Africa. His father had interests in a mine there and had also been negotiating to buy into some platinum mine in the north of the country, but Alan had never shown an interest in being involved in the mining industry.

Apparently, Alan was a bit of a rebel as far as his father was concerned. He had never had the desire to go to university after completing his schooling, nor did he want to join his father's financial company, so instead he became a journalist. Alan was the complete antithesis of what an upper-middle class young man should be like or what was expected of him, according to Mike. During their conversations, Mike had learned that Alan enjoyed music, but not any music. What delighted Alan more than anything was to turn the volume up high on his Hi-fi and get into some music, heavy metal music. Rock wouldn't have surprised Mike, but heavy metal didn't seem to fit in with the image of this young, gay, sophisticated man. Here was a clean-cut, good-looking, well-built young man who had everything going for him, yet he liked heavy metal rock. To Mike, heavy metal music was the epitome of roughness, drugs and wildness. Was Mike being judgmental in stereotyping Alan? Not all gay guys liked classical or club music, so Alan should be allowed to enjoy heavy metal music.

"Have you ever been to a heavy metal or rock concert?" asked Alan, grinning at Mike who looked surprised at this musical revelation.

"No, never. It's never interested me."

"You should give it a try sometime. You don't know what you're missing until you've tried it," laughed Alan. "In fact, there's a concert coming up next week; would you like to go?"

"You mean with you?"

"Sure. You might really enjoy it."

"I don't know," was Mike's embarrassed reply. He never saw himself as a rock music fan, but also wasn't about to divulge his lack of musical know-how. He could see Alan's look of despondency at his reply, so quickly added, "Maybe if I heard some of the music first I might consider going if I liked what I heard."

"Maybe we should go back to my place and I'll put on some *Iron Maiden, Metallica* or *Manowar* for you."

"Man oh who?"

"*Manowar*! They're an American metal group who've been around for years. I think you might like their music; to me their music's pure, especially when played loud," he giggled.

"But when it's loud isn't it difficult to hear the lyrics?" asked Mike with a little trepidation in his voice.

"It has to be loud," laughed Alan. "That's the way to enjoy it. It like gets into your blood and soon you're getting high on it."

"You mean like a drug?"

"You could say that, except this is a harmless drug."

"But tell me Alan, why do you like heavy metal music?"

"I suppose it's because it's rough, hard and almost anti-establishment, you might say," replied Alan.

"Do you see yourself as being anti-establishment?" enquired Mike.

"Not entirely; it's just that it makes me feel that when I'm listening to heavy metal music I can break free from the constraints of my family and their conformism."

Mike was a little surprised by Alan's comments, but both men continued to discuss their various tastes in music, entertainment and pleasure in life as they drank their beers.

"What sort of music do you like, Mike?" enquired Alan.

"I suppose you could say I have Catholic tastes in music, except for heavy metal, which I've never really listened to."

Mike began to see another side to Alan, a side that seemed to want to break free but was constrained by the pressures of his family. Alan was an only child and therefore had been spoiled as a very young boy. Whatever he wanted seemed to have been granted to him, but fortunately, in Mike's opinion, this had not continued into later life. Alan didn't seem to be a demanding person, but a soul living a double life: one for his parents and one for himself. Alan's apartment reflected his parents' influence, but Mike wanted to get to know the real Alan, the one that lay hidden under the skin of this beautiful young man.

Mike, on the other hand, had grown up in a very average, lower middle class family where they often went without material objects, but remained happy. Mike considered his own past. His father had been a successful plumber and his mother was a housewife. He had an older sister and a much younger brother who was still at school. All told, they were what would be considered a very ordinary family.

Mike, like Alan, had also not had the urge to go to university after school, but was far more interested in sport and wanted a career in that area. Both his parents were understanding and never inflicted their wishes on him. They felt that whatever Mike wanted to do in life, they would support, so when he left school, he started attending a gym and slowly built up his physique. He was proud of his body and enjoyed the admiration shown by others towards his physical shape, which was not in the same class as the competitive bodybuilders.

When he was twenty-two, Mike had left home and moved into his own apartment. This enabled him to have the freedom he so desired, the freedom to socialize with whomever he liked and go wherever and whenever he wanted. He had moved from Canterbury to London and enjoyed the big city life that abounded. Many a Friday or Saturday evening he would take to the streets of London, have some drinks in a pub and then wander on to one of the many clubs that he frequented, not so much for the music, but more for the company of others. On these excursions, he seldom went home alone after a night out. Mike was one of those people who never had to try to pick someone up for the night; they just seemed to flock to him and the choice was his. However, having said that, it must also be noted that Mike was selective about whom he took home.

"Last rounds!" was the cry from the barman.

As 'last rounds' was called in the pub, Mike offered to drive Alan home. When they arrived back at Alan's apartment, Mike switched off the engine and they sat for a while chatting in Mike's car.

"Alan, I've had a wonderful evening with you and I hope we can do this again some time, but in the meantime I want you to think about what happened at the gym today and if you remember anything else that you haven't already told me, please let me know because I want to get to the bottom of this mystery."

Although Alan could not think of anything else that he might have forgotten to tell Mike, he agreed to think about it, and then alighted from the car after having given Mike a thank-you kiss on the cheek. Mike smiled at the simplicity of the gesture, started up his car, tooted the car's horn and drove off in the direction of his home, but as he drove, his mind returned to thoughts of both Alan and the mysterious guy from the gym.

His mind was in turmoil. He really liked Alan and felt that he would like to make love to him, but then he fantasized about the strong, blonde hunk from the gym and he felt the urge to be wanted by him. Did he want to be the dominant one in a relationship with the likes of Alan or did he want to be dominated by someone whom he regarded as stronger and more powerful than himself? Both sounded exciting to him.

Chapter 6
MEETING WITH BRETT

Mike arrived back at his apartment, unlocked his front door, walked in and checked his voice mail on his answering machine. There were a few unimportant messages from friends, and then he heard Brett's voice.

"Hi, buddy. I might have some information for us. Meet me tomorrow outside the Half Price Ticket Booth in Leicester Square at 12.30p.m."

It was already late, so Mike decided not to phone Brett back to find out what he'd found, but rather wait until lunchtime the following day.

The following morning when Mike went into work, he spoke to Steven and asked if he could take his lunch break from 12.15 to 13.15 instead of his normal times. Steven was a little reluctant at first, but then said that he had no objection and didn't enquire as to why Mike wanted to change his lunch times, and so as the time neared, Mike caught the underground train from Holborn station to Leicester Square. He made his way to the Half Price Ticket Booth and waited for Brett.

It was another beautiful summer's day and the queues of people outside the ticket booth waiting to purchase theatre tickets extended some way around the perimeter of the park. The small park itself was crowded both with tourists and locals, enjoying the warmth of the sun and their lunch. Mike stood there in his sweat pants and T-shirt, watching the passing crowds of locals and tourists and reading the titles of the various theatrical shows on display. He could hear various accents from the people in the queues and wondered where some of them came from. Among these tongues of Babel, he heard a familiar voice. Brett was standing next to him.

"Admiring the view, buddy?"

"Just watching the passing trade," replied Mike, with a grin.

"Listen, let's go for a walk. I think I might have something for us."

The two men set off slowly in the direction of Charing Cross Station, with the sun streaming down on their bodies and the traffic roaring around them as they walked.

"I went onto our computer at the office after I left you at the gym and I found something that might be of importance," said Brett, taking a swig from a cold drink which he'd brought with him.

"Did you find out who the guy was?" asked Mike excitedly.

"No, not necessarily, but we might be onto something else."

As they continued to walk in the sunshine, Brett filled in Mike with all the information that he had managed to obtain from the computer.

Just as the tempo of traffic sped past them, so a similar tempo of words flowed from Brett as he excitedly related his news.

There had been a major robbery in Manchester one and a half years earlier and two of the criminals had been caught, but one was still on the run, as far as the local police knew. Brett had managed to contact the police in Manchester to enquire about the convicted men and the man on the run, and the police were going to try to find out any other information for him.

Brett and Mike eventually reached the Embankment and stood watching the Thames flow slowly past them. The sun glistened on the water, creating a glare that almost blinded them as they watched the small boats chug up and down the river, and the warmth of the sun began to make both men sweat. As Mike stared at the glistening river, he thought of Alan and being in his apartment and watching the same twinkling river gliding past.

"What's the significance of this robbery information?" enquired Mike, coming back to the here and now.

"It's a slim chance, but apparently the missing guy might fit the description of your mystery man," responded Brett with an air of excitement in his voice.

Mike stood staring at the slowness of the Thames. Who was this man that he had actually found attractive in a rough sort of way? Why was he in the gym showers and didn't seem to appear anywhere else? Where did he come from and why had he approached two guys who both just happened to be gay? At least he wasn't aware of any reports of the mysterious guy making a play for straight guys.

While they were standing watching the flow of water, the boats and the people, Brett's mobile phone rang. He answered it and as he spoke, so he glanced at Mike.

"Hello… yes… that's right. Where did you say?"

Mike saw the look in Brett's eyes and the slow grin beginning to form on his face.

"Right…thank you very much, I'll deal with it then… yes, thanks. Bye."

When he had finished speaking and switched his phone off he looked at Mike and said with a tinge of delight in his voice, "There seems to be a link with Berlin."

"What do you mean Berlin? The guy was here in London in the gym, so how can he be in Berlin?"

"That was Manchester," replied Brett. "They've found some connection with the missing guy in Berlin. Apparently, the last they heard of the guy was that he was in Berlin."

"But if we're talking about the same person, and if it is the guy who was in the gym, both I and Alan saw him here in London," continued Mike. "I don't understand what's going on."

"Listen, when I get back to the office, I'll call Manchester again and see if I can get more details, then I'll get back to you and we can take it from there."

They bought themselves something to eat and then both Mike and Brett started heading towards Charing Cross underground where they caught their trains back to work.

Back at the gym, Mike phoned Alan and told him what Brett had found, but it was equally strange to Alan that the police attached an importance to Berlin, yet both men had encountered the guy in the gym in London.

While they were on the phone, Alan said: "I wondered if you'd like to come round tonight and listen to a bit of heavy metal music so that you're a little more prepared for the concert next week."

Mike laughed and said, "You're really determined to educate me aren't you?"

Alan merely giggled on the other end of the telephone line, but he wanted to see Mike again, not only to play him his favorite music, but to see him as well. Alan was developing stronger feelings for Mike.

Mike also liked the idea of seeing this virile young man again so soon, and so did his slowly engorging cock, but not necessarily listening to heavy metal. As he spoke to Alan, he wasn't thinking specifically of the music, but rather the 'music' that they could create with each other. Without thinking, he said: "Is that all you had in mind?"

The words just seemed to tumble from his mouth and it was too late to put them back in.

Alan merely laughed again at the other end of the line. "You never know," was the giggled reply.

"I'm sorry, I didn't mean it like that," apologized Mike.

"Why are you apologizing?" asked Alan.

"Well I'm standing here talking to you and I must confess that I've got the most enormous hard-on," whispered Mike, as he spoke the last words.

Alan laughed even louder over the phone.

"I like the sound of that," he said, "but I must confess, so have I, so in that case I think you'd better come round tonight. Would seven o'clock suit you?"

"Sure, that'd be great. See you later then."

Mike put down the phone, looked around to see if anyone was watching and then put his hand into the front of his sweat pants and adjusted the position of his throbbing cock.

Mike made his way back into the weights area and set about helping some of the guys training. Knowing that he was going round to Alan's that evening, made him almost excited. It wasn't that he never received invitations to people's homes, but he really was beginning to like Alan a great deal, and he was really looking forward to spending the evening with him. This in itself was a little strange to Mike, as he had usually gone for older guys, but now he wasn't thinking about their age differences any more.

Alan was not like most of the other bodybuilders. He came to the gym to keep in shape and not to bulk up his body. In fact Alan's body shape was lean, yet he had one of the most beautiful six-packs Mike had ever seen. Even the most ardent of bodybuilders had made mention of Alan's abdominal muscles and how well-defined they were. Mike felt proud to know that he had been partly responsible for Alan achieving his abs.

The loudspeaker in the gym cut into Mike's thoughts when it bellowed out: "Telephone at reception for Mike Schwantz."

Mike sauntered past the other personal trainers who were working with their various clients, towards the reception area where the phone call was waiting for him. He picked up the receiver.

"Mike Schwantz speaking."

"Hi Mike, it's Brett here. Do you fancy a weekend in Berlin next week?"

"Why what the hell are you up to now?"

"Just answer my question. Do you want to go to Berlin next weekend?"

"Sounds great but why and who's paying?"

"To investigate, in answer to your first question and you are paying, in answer to your second," came the reply.

"I'm not paying for both of us; and is it just you and me who are going?"

"Yes. Are you up for it?"

"Sure. When do we leave?"

"Friday evening at 6.00p.m and return on Sunday afternoon at 3.00p.m."

There was a click and Mike was left holding the phone. That was the end of the conversation, short and sweet, and he was now completely confused. He had seen the man in London; now they were jet-setting off to Berlin. What the hell was going on? As he replaced the receiver, he wondered what Brett had found out and why the urgency to go to Berlin. Then he thought of Alan and wondered whether he should mention any of his conversation with Brett to him, after all, Alan had also been involved with the mystery man.

Chapter 7
A SEXUAL MUSICAL EVENING

The doorbell to Alan's apartment rang and Mike waited for the door to open. There was no response. He waited a while longer and then rang again. The solid oak door opened slowly and there stood Alan like Mike had never seen before.

"Come in Mike. Great to see you again," said the beaming young man.

Mike stared at Alan, speechless. He couldn't believe what he was seeing; he was transfixed.

"You look surprised, Mike. Anything wrong?" said Alan nonchalantly.

Mike wasn't quite sure what to say, and then he said: "You look stunning," his eyes twinkling and a broad smile developing across his face.

"Do you mean it or are you having me on?"

"It's not what I expected from you, but you look great in that."

Mike knew Alan looked great in any outfit, but the outfit that Alan was now wearing was exceptional because he could feel an arousal in his groin area, just like the mercury in a thermometer would rise on a hot day.

"So are you going to stand at the door all night or are you coming in?"

Alan led the way into the lounge with Mike following like a puppy dog, watching Alan's trim ass move gently within the tight confines of a pair of leather jeans. Alan's sturdy, long legs looked even sexier with the leather wrapped tightly around them, and his bubble-butt seemed to be molded into the material. When they got to the lounge, Alan turned to face Mike. Mike surveyed the sight in front of him. Alan had on a leather harness, which enhanced his abs and chest, and his tight leather jeans. Mike was fascinated by the sight before him; it tended to contradict the décor which surrounded them; the furnishings so elegant and meticulously placed and here was this young man looking rough but sexy. Rugged leather clothing and Louis XIV furniture didn't seem to go together. He had never experienced anything like this before, but he was finding out that the sight of this young man in leather was a real turn-on. He desperately wanted to touch – no, feel – no, grab at the young man; to grasp that firm leather encased butt, tear the leather from his body and ram his cock into that waiting ass.

"Please don't think me rude, but why are you dressed like this?" Mike politely asked, walking around Alan and surveying the inviting sight.

"I wanted you to experience the full heavy metal feeling. If you were to see *Manowar* you'd see that they are also into leather, so I wanted to look the part as well as feel it."

"Well I must admit it was a bit of a shock seeing you like this, but I really like it and I must confess that I think it makes you look even sexier. Mmm, and the smell of that leather turns me on," said Mike, sniffing the air.

"Thanks, Mike, I appreciate the compliment."

"But tell me, what would your mother say if she saw you now?"

Alan burst out laughing.

"She'd probably have a fit or something. She knows nothing of this side of me."

"And what side would that be?"

"I'm not impartial to a bit of leather, you know, and I'm not referring to furniture."

"Do you often dress like this?" enquired Mike, hoping that this might become a regular occurrence.

"Only when I feel like being turned on," joked Alan. "I'm just teasing you.

Sometimes when I go to a metal gig, I wear them."

"In that case I might just come with you … to the concert."

"But I'm not into leather in the sense of S&M," continued Alan. "I have seen pictures of guys in slings and things like that, being screwed by leather guys, and I found it a turn-on, but I've never seen myself as being involved in something like that. How about you?"

Mike stammered as he tried to answer Alan's question.

"I don't know. I've never tried it, but yes, I agree with you, it could be interesting, the leather clothing side of it, I mean; not the painful side though."

"No I don't think I'd like someone beating me with whips or chains," continued Alan. "I'm not into pain; I prefer a firm but loving scene with a guy."

In the lounge, Alan had beers ready in the lounge and when they were seated, he leaned over to the Hi-fi and put on a *Manowar* CD.

"This is especially for you, to ease you into a little heavy metal," said Alan grinning impishly at Mike.

"I thought we'd start with something easy – something that you might appreciate."

The music was the classical piece *Nessun Dorma* from the opera *Turandot,* but sung by a true heavy metal singer, Eric Adams. Mike knew this piece of music and sat there silently listening to a man's voice attack the high notes with gusto without any trace of effort. Alan watched him with a smile of his face and Mike became aware of Alan's stare.

When the singer got to that part of the music where the chorus joins in and the extremely high notes were nearing, tears began to well up in Mike's eyes. The sound was beautiful and having Alan sitting there with him was equally beautiful. His emotions were running high just looking at Alan. Suddenly the song ended and there was silence. The two men sat staring at each other, but neither spoke.

"Wow!" exclaimed Mike eventually, wiping a tear from his eye. "I've never heard anything like that before. It sent chills down my spine hearing that piece."

"I told you that you might like heavy metal."

"But that's not what I expected."

"You're right; heavy metal is not all like that. This band is exceptional. They take risks with their music and it pays off. I'll play you something else by them which is totally different."

Alan clicked on the remote and chose another track. The sound blasted from the speakers and Mike's expression on his face showed that this was now what he expected heavy metal music to sound like: loud and destructive.

Alan stretched out on the easy chair opposite from Mike and folded his arms, his feet keeping tempo with the beat of the music. The music blared forth and Mike watched Alan go into a trance-like state as he listened to the music, then he noticed Alan run his thumbs casually over his bare nipples as the band played on. Mike found himself becoming aroused at seeing this. He found it awkward to sit comfortably on the couch because of his arousal and had to constantly keep adjusting his position. Alan became aware of Mike's awkwardness so he offered a solution.

"Why don't you take them off if they're worrying you?" he shouted above the noise of the music.

"I beg your pardon?" came the equally loud reply.

"Your jeans; take them off if you'd feel more comfortable," shouted Alan,

miming the removal of his jeans.

Mike hesitated at first, thinking of where this might lead, then stretched out his legs in front of him and started to unbutton his jeans. His white Calvin Klein briefs burst into view. Alan watched with interest. Mike pushed his jeans down to his ankles then bent over to undo his trainers. He kicked them off and Alan helped him to pull off his jeans. Mike sat back against the cool back of the couch, his crotch thrusting skywards, still safely enclosed in his Calvin Klein's.

"Don't you feel better now?" asked Alan, turning down the volume of the music and standing legs spread apart in front of Mike.

"A bit," replied Mike trying to push his swollen cock down in the hopes that he would lose his erection.

"I don't think that's going to help," suggested Alan, staring at the bulging front of Mike's briefs; "but take your shirt off too, if you like," he smiled.

Admiring Alan's body in front of him, Mike didn't need a second invitation. He pulled his T-shirt over his head and threw it on the couch next to him. He stretched out there in his white socks and white briefs with Alan standing seductively in front of him, thumbs hooked into the waistband of his leather jeans.

"Do you feel more comfortable now?"

"Much better thanks."

Alan moved closer to Mike and placed his knees on the couch on either side of Mike's legs. He then lowered his leather-bound ass so that it just touched Mike's crotch. Alan slowly slid his ass over the length of Mike's cock, allowing it to slide over the crack between his leather-bound ass cheeks. Mike felt the leather rub over his cock and then felt the throb of his swollen, almost exploding dick. Alan continued to rub up and down Mike's cock and then started to nip gently at Mike's nipples with his teeth. Mike, by this time was groaning loudly as the young man continued to arouse his older friend. Neither spoke but just looked lustfully into each other's eyes. Mike reciprocated by getting hold of Alan's nipples and pulling him closer towards his own chest. Alan gasped as he neared Mike's mouth and then felt the urgency of Mike's mouth encompass his own. Tongue fought tongue as Mike tried to insert his tongue deeper into Alan's mouth, their lips crushing together.

As the music's tempo increased, so did theirs. There was no finesse in their actions, rather, animalistic craving between the two men. Mike rolled Alan onto his back on the couch and proceeded to suck on his nipples, licking them and nipping at their swollenness. Mike slid down Alan's muscular stomach, kissing and licking it as he descended towards Alan's crotch. He reached the top of Alan's leather jeans and unbuckled them; then he slowly undid the zip. He breathed in and caught the clean, fresh smell of leather and Alan's body. He placed his hands under Alan's tight butt and lifted Alan's hips and eased off his leathers, allowing the long, beautiful manhood to break free.

Pre-come oozed from the slit in Alan's cock. Rather than waste it, Mike extended his tongue and with its tip, gently licked it away. He flicked his tongue in and out of the piss-slit, causing Alan to groan and writhe with pleasure. Mike let his tongue run down the underside vein of Alan's throbbing cock until it reached Alan's softly furred balls and kissed each gently.

Mike was now in a trance and both men were oblivious to the music playing. All Mike wanted to hear were the satisfied groans of Alan. He lapped up Alan's silky balls, taking one at a time into the warmth of his mouth and rolling his tongue gently around each one, soaking the soft fluff of hair in warm saliva and kissing them lovingly.

Mike gently rubbed a forefinger over the pulsing entrance to Alan's beautiful ass, then slowly began to insert one finger and felt the muscles around Alan's ass clamp tightly onto his finger. He continued to relish Alan's balls and cock as he slowly continued his finger's journey into the darkness of Alan's interior. Alan's groaning became louder and Mike felt him push down onto his finger. Mike slowly withdrew his finger and felt Alan's muscles tighten in an effort to try to prevent him from leaving. He now slowly inserted a second finger. When Alan felt this, his grinding became more intensified. Mike spread his fingers inside Alan and tickled his innards. Alan gasped when he felt the fingers stretching him.

"Please fuck me Mike, please," gasped Alan.

Mike ignored the request, as he wanted Alan to enjoy every moment. A feeling of power came over Mike. His mouth resumed working up and down the length of Alan's cock, rolling his tongue around the head. The only sound that was obvious to Mike was the increased volume of Alan's groans of pleasure.

"Please Mike, I need you inside me," wailed Alan.

Mike removed his hold on Alan and felt for his jeans on the floor and pulled out a condom. He tore open the foil, pulled down his Calvin Klein's and placed the condom on the tip of his cock. Slowly he unrolled it over his throbbing cock and stood up. He lifted Alan's legs and placed each over his shoulders. He squeezed some lube onto his fingers and inserted them into the warmth of Alan's ass, readying him for his advances. He slid Alan to the edge of the couch and positioned his bargepole at the waiting entrance. Mike watched as his cock-head touched the opening to Alan's ass. The pink hole winked at him in anticipation. Alan desperately wanted Mike to slide into him. Mike exerted a little pressure and watched his cock-head break through the barrier and enter about an inch or two. Alan sighed loudly, smiled contentedly and pushed down on Mike's cock.

"Take me I'm all yours. Please."

A deep guttural groan echoed around the lounge as Alan forced himself onto Mike's cock, taking his whole length into the warmth of his tight, cute ass. A slow push and withdrawal action proceeded, just as their chests rose and fell with their passionate breathing. Mike pushed deeply into Alan, leaning across him so that their lips became conjoined. Their tongues made contact just as Mike's cock rubbed up against Alan's prostate. Mike heard and felt the gasp from Alan's mouth, and as the music of the hi-fi increased in volume and intensity, so did that of the two men.

Mike began to increase his rhythmic thrusts as he felt the tightness surround his cock. He could feel himself nearing the edge of no return. His muscular body loomed over that of Alan's as he ploughed into the willing young man's tender ass.

"I'm getting close, Alan," said Mike, pounding furiously, balls slapping onto Alan's ass.

"So am I. I'm going to come," shouted Alan, above the guitar riffs and drum thuds of the music.

The crescendo of the music was complemented only by the groans and sighs coming from Alan and Mike. As their thrusts lessened, and with perspiration dripping from each man, they collapsed on the couch together, arm in arm, oblivious of the music from the hi-fi; the only music that was of importance to them was the singing in their hearts for each other, which slowly ebbed to sleep.

Chapter 8
BERLIN

Mike and Alan attended the music concert during the week, but Mike admitted that he'd gone simply to please Alan and because of his feelings for him and not because of the music. Mike had agreed that some heavy metal music, albeit very little in his opinion, was tolerable, but it was more for Alan that he'd agreed to go. Alan was in his element at the concert, dressed in his leather jeans and T-shirt, rocking to the music, and looking sexy in Mike's estimation. Mike admired his friend's enthusiasm, enjoying his happiness.

The music was predictably loud and Mike spent most of the evening watching the audience, rather than the various bands on stage, and getting his enjoyment from their antics, especially those who were enjoying themselves in the mosh-pit. Alan, however, appreciated his friend being there and the sense of freedom that he was enjoying. It was a feeling of escapism from the confines of his 'stuffy' apartment.

Alan sang along with the bands as they played, moving his body to the rhythm of the music and waving his arms in the air in time to the music. Mike had never experienced anything like this before and although he was immersed in the mass of bodies and noise, he never felt embarrassed by Alan's antics; in fact it brought him closer to his friend.

On Friday, Brett met Mike and they made their way to Heathrow Airport to catch their flight to Berlin. Mike had told Alan what was happening and that he'd be away for the weekend, but if he found out anything in Berlin, he'd call him.

They boarded the flight and set off for Berlin. The flight was uneventful, the aircraft stewards were dull and the flight was over fairly quickly. On the plane, Mike had sat back and asked Brett what their plans were.

"Tomorrow morning we're going to meet a guy who might be able to help us. I've booked us into a hotel in the city center and he's going to meet us there."

"Who is this guy?" asked Mike.

"He's a cop and he apparently knows something about the missing guy from the robbery."

"You mean the one who looks like our mysterious man?"

"That's it, but until then we're free to enjoy Berlin and what it has to offer."

"I suppose that means letting your hair down now that you're not with Belinda?" joked Mike, jabbing his buddy in the ribs.

"Listen buddy, whatever happens this weekend is strictly between you and me, and certainly not Belinda. Okay?"

"Anything you say, boss. It's a deal," replied Mike, not quite knowing what Brett had in mind.

They arrived in Berlin and caught a cab to the hotel in Nürnbergerstrasse where their hotel was situated. Having booked into their hotel, they quickly unpacked the limited clothing that they had brought with them and then Brett suggested they go and have something to eat and drink as it was early evening. They found a local restaurant where they had a pleasant meal together, and then went in search of a pub for a drink. They found one near the hotel where a number of men and women were in festive mood.

Music was blaring from a hi-fi situated somewhere in the bar and to counteract the volume of the music; everyone was obliged to shout to one another when speaking. Mike and Brett ordered a couple of drinks at the bar and settled down to watch some of the locals.

"How are things with you and Belinda?" enquired Mike, rather loudly.

"Oh, you know, we have our ups and downs, like any relationship."

"But how serious are you two about getting married?"

"Shit, she can't wait, but I don't want to rush into it just yet," commented Brett, taking a swig of his German pilsner. "She keeps dropping hints, but I usually change the subject as best I can. It's not that I don't love her, it's just that I don't think I'm ready for marriage."

"You mean you still want to sow your wild oats?"

"I suppose you could say that; but what about you?"

Mike smiled on being asked this question.

"What about me?" asked Mike.

"When are you going to get married?"

"Never!" came the sharp retort. "I'm not the marrying kind; you should know that; besides I like to play the field."

"But I'm sure you'd like to settle down with someone one day?" remarked Brett, taking another swig of his drink.

"Oh sure. When I meet the right person."

"And is there anyone at the moment that we know of?"

"Maybe, but I'm not committing," said Mike smiling to himself and thinking of his and Alan's last night together.

"Do I know her?" enquired Brett.

Mike was tempted to rebut this question, but he thought otherwise about it. He could have said something like, 'It's not *her* but *him*'; but then he wasn't entirely sure how Brett would take it. Although they'd known each other for years, Mike was still in the closet, so to speak, to his colleagues and family.

They ordered a couple more drinks and then decided to call it a night as they were both tired and needed to get up early the next morning.

The following morning, after breakfast, they waited in the foyer of the hotel for their contact.

"Do you know what this guy looks like?" asked Mike, with a little apprehension in his voice.

"Not really," came the reply, "but when he arrives I'm sure that we'll know."

"Some cop you are," laughed Mike, "not knowing what our contact looks like."

The two men sat there for over an hour waiting. People came and went, but no one who looked like a contact, whatever a contact looks like, came near them. After about an hour and a half, a young man of about twenty-five or six, dressed in black jeans and a black T-shirt wandered into the hotel foyer. He was short and stocky with tousled brown hair and a day's beard growth. He looked around the foyer as if searching for someone. Brett spotted him and said, "This could be our man."

Brett rose from his seat and crossed over to the young man.

"Guten morgen. Are you here to see me?" asked Brett, offering a hand to shake.

"You are Brett from England?"

"Yes, and you are Thomas?"

"Zat is right," replied the young German.

"I'm so glad to meet you."

Thomas smiled openly as Brett escorted him back to where we had been sitting. The young man had dark, brooding eyes, but this didn't detract from his masculine presence, open face and rugged good looks.

"Thomas, this is a friend of mine called Mike. Mike this is Thomas. He's an undercover cop here in Berlin."

The two men greeted each other and Mike felt the firm grip of the young German's handshake. He looked into the brooding eyes and smiled. The smile on Thomas's face broadened as he took a seat next to Mike.

Mike watched the young German with interest. He looked at the young man's face and stocky body, but it was his unshaven look that appealed to Mike because it gave its owner a more rugged look about him. Mike noticed how relaxed the German appeared as he sat casually in the seat next to him. Most of the conversation was taking place between Brett and Thomas, with Mike adding the odd comment. Mike noticed that Thomas's attention focused more on Brett, but every now and again, Thomas smiled at Mike, his dark eyes twinkling every time he did so. Mike also sensed warmth emanating from Thomas as they sat in close proximity of each other.

Drinks were ordered, delivered and Mike sat watching Thomas with great interest over the top of his beer glass. The more he paid attention to him, the more Mike found his rough look appealing. On one occasion, their feet touched and again Thomas merely smiled at Mike, without showing objection to what had occurred. However, Mike wasn't sure whether Brett had noticed anything between them, but it didn't seem to worry him unduly.

"Can you tell us what you know about this mysterious man, Thomas?" asked Brett.

In broken English, Thomas replied: "All I know is zat ze robbery vas unsuccessful and ze vun man got away. Vee ver told zat he vas here in Berlin, but no vun knew ver. Zen I managed to get somezing from an informer. I have asked zis informer to meet us tonight if zat is agreeable to you."

"Of course," replied Brett, excitedly. "The sooner we can solve this mystery the better."

"Brett tells me you ver ze unfortunate person, Mike?" he asked turning his full attention to Mike and smiling his engaging smile.

"Well I suppose so," he said, but muttered under his breath, "I wouldn't call it unfortunate, not with that body!"

"Zis man apparently had a tattoo on ze arm and a scar above ze eye, ja?"

"Yes," replied Mike, "and he was extremely well built, bigger than me."

"Ja, zis sounds like our man," continued Thomas, grinning at Mike.

"Where are we to meet your contact this evening?" interrupted Brett.

"It is not far from here. Zer is a club in Fuggerstrasse. It opens at 11.00 p.m. Vee are to meet him at midnight zer. You can of course get zer earlier if you vish, as zer is also a bar and a movie-shop to vich you can visit, should you want to drink and see videos."

Mike smiled to himself when he heard Thomas's instructions, not only because he thought of the movie-shop, which could prove quite interesting if it had porno movies, although he wasn't quite sure how Brett would react, but also he was looking forward to seeing how the Germans partied. He mused on all that had been said and wondered what his weekend in Berlin held in store for him, but better still, what did it hold for Brett, because to Mike, a place which had a movie-shop attached to a club sounded very gay to him, so what was Brett going to do?

After Thomas had given them instructions on how to get to the club, Mike and Brett went for a tour of the city to get their bearings and see some of the sights, both cultural and human. In the afternoon, the two men went back to their hotel and decided to have a rest as their night was going to be a long one.

The hotel room was simply furnished, as average hotels usually are, but instead of being given a twin bedded room, they had a room with a double bed and a couch.

On their first night in Berlin, Brett had chosen to sleep on the couch while Mike had the bed. When they returned in the afternoon from their walk around the city, they both collapsed exhausted onto the bed to watch some TV. Mike and Brett lay side by side, staring up at the TV, which was attached to a bracket high up on the wall opposite to the bed, until they both eventually fell asleep.

At approximately eight o'clock in the evening, Mike opened his eyes and saw that it was beginning to get dark outside. He continued to lie on the bed, but noticed that while he had been asleep, Brett must have got up and stripped himself of his clothes, because he now lay naked on the bed, still fast asleep. Mike looked at Brett's naked, lithe body and felt an urge to touch his friend. He looked so peaceful lying there, curled up next to Mike.

Mike's eyes traced down Brett's body, taking in the angelic face to the well shaped chest, the firm stomach and then on to the flaccid, long cock that lay there waiting to be awakened. Mike looked at the stem of Brett's cock, which was not as thick as his own, and saw a thick vein running along its length. His eyes moved up to the tip of Brett's cock and he saw the most beautifully mushroomed-shaped head. He lay there visualizing his mouth encircling that big head, filling his mouth with Brett's manhood and bringing his friend to a climax, but then he thought of Belinda, Brett's girlfriend. He wondered whether she ever gave Brett blowjobs and whether Brett in fact, would allow a man to bring pleasure to him. Mike had never really taken such notice of his friend's body before. He remembered when they were growing up how they would shower together after sports matches and splash and horseplay under the showers, but now that they had grown into men, both their bodies had developed and Mike admired what he saw lying there.

Bret stirred and adjusted his position on the bed. He turned onto his back and Mike watched as Brett's cock lay casually across the left side of his belly. Mike tentatively and slowly adjusted his own position on the bed sliding down it until he was close to Brett's pelvic area. He lay and admired Brett's gently rising and falling stomach, as he breathed. Mike was so tempted to touch Brett, but was unsure of what Brett's reaction would be. He leant closer and then, very softly and quietly, he began to blow onto Brett's cock. It wasn't so much blowing as breathing. His warm breath made Brett's cock begin to stir. Mike could see the stem move its position uncontrollably and he could see the start of an erection forming. As he watched intently, so his own cock began swelling inside his Calvin Klein's. Mike continued to breathe gently onto Brett's manhood, watching it grow in length and thickness, but still afraid to actually touch it in case Brett awoke and was offended.

Brett sighed softly and Mike stopped his action, waiting to see if Brett woke up, but he didn't. Mike resumed his action, but as he did so, Brett's legs began to spread apart. Mike climbed gingerly from the bed, picked up a tube of lube and moved around to position him between Brett's legs. He slid slowly up the bed until his mouth was close to Brett's balls. He tentatively flicked out his tongue so that the tip could just touch Brett's ball sac. He noticed how the testicle jumped. He waited for a reaction from Brett, but there was none, so he repeated his action on the other testicle and then gently kissed each one. As his tongue began to lather Brett's balls, so Brett's legs spread wider, allowing Mike more access to the area under Brett's balls. He licked his index finger and ran it slowly over the length of Brett's throbbing cock. When his finger reached the tip of Brett's cock, he felt the tell-tale man-juice oozing from its tip. He wiped it with his finger and then placed that finger into his mouth. He ran his tongue over its stickiness, enjoying his friend's sweet taste.

Mike slid a little further up the bed so that his mouth was positioned over Brett's twitching cock. Still there was no reaction from Brett, who lay 'asleep'. Mike opened his mouth and in one swift move, had engulfed the whole of Brett's cock, stem and head. He held it in his warmth while Brett groaned on the bed. He felt Brett thrust upwards as he slowly began to thrust into Mike's mouth. This was the moment that Mike had been waiting for, the invitation to go further.

Brett's eyes flickered open and Mike looked up from his position and smiled as best he could with a mouth full of cock.

"Please don't stop, Mike," whispered Brett.

Mike had no intention of doing so. He slid his mouth slowly up and down Brett's length luxuriating at the taste of his manhood. Mike swirled his tongue around the mushroom head, gently inserting his tongue into Brett's piss-slit. Brett bucked upwards, lifting his ass off the bed. Mike took this opportunity to cup both palms of his hands on Brett's buttocks. He pulled each cheek apart and let his fingers wander towards Brett's pink rose. Mike rubbed a finger around the entrance to Brett's ass, feeling the small rose entrance quiver and as it did so, so Brett's cock throbbed in his mouth. He removed one hand and put some of the lube onto his middle finger; then he proceeded gently to insert his finger back into Brett's waiting passage.

Brett was so relaxed that he never fought Mike's entry, but gasped loudly as the finger slowly slid into the dark recesses of his being. Brett pushed down on Mike's finger. The finger stroked inside and Brett groaned even more. Mike gently pulled his finger out towards the exit and felt Brett clamp tightly around it so as to prevent him from leaving, but Mike had no intention of doing that. Instead, two fingers began a journey to pleasure.

Brett felt some pain but it was not unpleasant. In fact it was bringing him closer to a tumultuous climax. Mike spread his fingers inside Brett and felt his nutty shaped prostate, which he gently began to rub. Brett sounded as though he were crying as he whimpered in ecstasy, writhing his body on the bed. All the while, Mike kept up his attack on Brett's dribbling cock.

"Mike, I'm not going to last much longer," whimpered Brett amidst groans and gasps.

"Oh fuck, I'm going to come," shouted Brett.

Mike prepared himself for the first onslaught of Brett's fountain of man juice. Brett fired a load into Mike's mouth which he began to swallow, but he couldn't keep up with the amount of cum that Brett was sending down his throat. Some dribbled out of the side of Mike's mouth as he pushed his fingers hard and roughly against Brett's prostate, causing Brett's whole body to quiver and shake with passion on the bed.

As Brett shot his final salvo into the warmth of Mike's mouth, Mike felt his buddy's body begin to relax. Mike sucked on Brett's cock in an effort to drain it dry. He tightened his lips around the stem and slowly dragged upwards, bringing with him the last remnants of Brett's seed. He gave the head a last twirl with his tongue and then when both of their breathing had returned to normality, Mike slipped his mouth from Brett's wet cock and slid himself up along Brett's body until they were face-to-face, whereupon Mike kissed Brett gently on the mouth. Brett reciprocated but with more intensity, inserting his tongue into Mike's mouth where he could taste the sweetness of his cum. Their tongues twisted together and Brett sucked hard on Mike's tongue as if to drain it of any of his remaining love-juice. When their mouths parted, the two friends smiled into each other's eyes.

"Thank you," whispered Brett. "I've always wanted to do something like that with you, but I've been afraid to say anything to you about it."

"I'm sorry, Brett, but I couldn't resist it as you lay there naked next to me."

"Do you do this often, Mike?"

"Do you mean am I gay?"

"Well if you put it like that, yes."

Mike appeared a little embarrassed by this question, but he had known Brett long enough to be honest with him.

"Sure, when we were young we both had girl friends and yes I screwed them, like you did, but as I got older I found I was becoming more attracted to guys, but I haven't come out to my family or the people I work with. If they have an idea about my sexuality, then they haven't said anything to me about it. But what about you?"

"I've never really been with a guy. Sure, I'd do a hand-job with other guys when I was very young, but that didn't count, because everybody was doing those things."

"Well, you didn't do it with me," retorted Mike, sounding envious. "But where does that put you with Belinda?"

"This was the first time with an adult guy, so remember, nothing to Belinda about this, buddy!"

"I won't say anything if you don't say anything," responded Mike, exhaustedly.

"But I owe you one."

"What do you mean you owe me one?" queried Mike.

"That was the greatest feeling I've ever had and you gave me enormous pleasure, but I did nothing for you and I've wanted to please you for years but have never had the courage to make a move on you."

"Well that means that we'll have to do something about that, won't we?" smirked Mike, rolling Brett over onto his stomach and slapping his tight ass and wondering where this now put them.

Chapter 9
DEEP IN THE CHAMBERS

Brett and Mike showered, dressed and set off by taxi for their meeting with Thomas at the club in Fuggerstrasse. They arrived at 11.30p.m, paid and went in. The place had quite a number of people there already, some dressed in leathers, and the music was loud, making Mike think of Alan and his heavy metal. They wandered around to survey the area and when they found the bar area, Thomas was already standing there waiting for them.

"I'm glad you found ze place," shouted Thomas, above the noise of the music. "It is noisy here, ja? Vee get our drinks zen vee go to a quiet place."

They ordered two beers and followed Thomas up a floor to a quieter lounge area where there were tables and chairs.

"This is much better," sighed Mike. "At least I can hear myself think," although he knew that Alan would disagree with him.

They sat down and Brett and Mike looked around them, surveying those people also sitting in the quieter part of the club. Mike felt the nearness of Brett as they pulled their chairs closer together. The warmth that glowed from his newfound closeness to Brett made Mike smile. Perhaps this might be the start of a different relationship between the two young men. He'd always fantasized about having some sort of relationship with a straight guy, or even in Brett's case, what can only be assumed as a bi-sexual guy. He knew that their friendship had been cemented many years ago, but maybe there might be something a little more intimate between them now that they had shown physical feelings towards each other. Maybe they could become fuck-buddies, if Brett was willing, thought Mike; that's if Mike was not in a serious relationship. That would be great, he thought. Brett would still have Belinda, but on those rare occasions, he could also have Mike. Mike's crotch began to itch at the thought.

"What's going through your mind?" said Brett leaning closer to Mike. "I can see the smile on your face and the bulge in your jeans," he whispered so that Thomas wouldn't overhear him.

Mike immediately looked down at his crotch; Brett was right, a bulge was forming. Mike met Brett's smiling gaze and smiled sheepishly.

"I think you know," was Mike's embarrassed response.

"Maybe later, buddy."

Fortunately for Mike, their whispered conversation was interrupted by the arrival of Thomas's contact. A tall, thin man of about thirty appeared at their table. He looked very ordinary; in fact one might not even give him a second glance if one passed him in a street, yet if one looked deeper, there certainly appeared a man who had an air of curiosity about him. Mike looked at the face and immediately smiled to himself. He nudged Brett and indicated towards the man.

"What does he look like to you?" asked Mike, sotto voce.

Brett gave the man a serious look.

"A cross between a rabbit and a shrew," came the whispered reply.

Mike gave a slight guffaw.

The man's face resembled a young shrew with its sharp, pointed nose, small narrow mouth, chin which receded into his throat suggesting the beginnings of a double chin, and protruding from the narrow lips, were two buck teeth.

The man gave Thomas a formal nod of his head and immediately sat down next to him, without actually being invited to do so. Mike's eyes suddenly lit up when he saw how the man was dressed. He was cloaked in leather. The sight brought memories rushing back into his mind of his night with Alan and how the sight and smell of the leather had turned him on. Was this to be another of those nights, he wondered?

"Gentlemen, zis is Heinz, a contact of mine. I have dealt vith him many times and his information has always been reliable, not so Heinz?"

"Ja!" came a high-pitched voice.

Mike and Brett looked at each other, ready to burst out laughing at this character.

The man noticed their reaction and merely gave a disinterested grunt.

"Vot can you tell zees men, Heinz?"

Heinz eyed Brett and Mike with suspicion and then looked to Thomas for reassurance. Thomas smiled at the man and nodded. This was obviously the signal that the two Englishmen could be trusted.

As Heinz spoke in his high-pitched voice with his accent, so his arms began to flay the air effeminately.

"Ze robbery zat you speak of did not have three men involved, but five." He emphasized the word 'five' and thumped his fist on the table as he said it, causing Mike to start suddenly.

"Five!" exclaimed Brett.

Heinz flashed him a filthy look and bared his buck teeth, for interrupting his story, but he nevertheless carried on.

"Two of ze men escaped. Ja! Von of ze men has a tattoo and a scar as you said, but ze other does not," he said, almost melodramatically.

"But if two escaped and two were captured, what happened to the fifth?" asked Brett, leaning closer to the contact.

Heinz stared into Brett's eyes, then squinted and tightened his lips as if to warn him not to interrupt again, paused and then said, as solemnly as his high-pitched voice could muster, "Ze fifth vas murdered!"

"Murdered?" echoed Mike. "But who killed him and why?"

"No von seems to know," came the reply as Heinz dramatically shrugged his shoulders, "but ze zinking on ze street is zat von of ze robbers did it." He pursed his lips as he gave this last bit of information

"Perhaps zer was greed involved," offered Thomas as a possible motive. "It often happens in cases such as robbery, not so Brett?"

"Yes you're right there. But now where does our tattooed friend from the gym fit in?"

"You mean, why is he always seen only at the gym?" asked Mike.

"Well yes, that's the puzzling part of this whole equation."

The group tried to fathom this dilemma out but without success. Brett turned once more to Heinz.

"We were told that this muscle-bound hunk had been seen in Germany, Berlin to be precise. Is that true?"

"Ooh Ja," replied Heinz with an effeminate lilt to his voice. "He had, but not recently. Vee do not know ver zis man is now."

"But what's the connection with Berlin?"

"Drugs!" exclaimed Thomas. At this point, Heinz's eyes lit up. "Zay must be dealing in drugs here in Germany and moving zem between Germany and England to market zem," continued Thomas.

"Maybe the muscle man is the courier," remarked Brett.

"That would make sense with regard to his trips between Germany and England, but what concerns me is that when I came face-to-face with the guy, it never entered my mind that he might do drugs or be involved in any way."

"You cannot easily tell, Mike. Zometimes it is extremely difficult to know if omeone is taking or dealing in drugs, especially the couriers; they often don't do ze drugs." Replied Thomas. "He may be innocent, but I doubt it."

"Do either of you know any of their names?" enquired Mike.

"No," answered Heinz in almost a disappointed squeal.

"Except the two who ver captured and are in prison," replied Thomas.

They had finished their drinks so Mike offered to get a refill for everyone. He rose and made his way to the bar. The music could still be heard thumping in the background and he could see many more people had ventured into the club since their arrival. He ordered the drinks and stood at the bar waiting. He surveyed the area and was pleasantly surprised to see how many good-looking young men there were. The dress code was varied with some men in jeans and many more in some form of leather attire, which was beginning to become a turn on for him. At one stage he even tried to visualize what Brett would look like in leathers. Bingo! His cock throbbed at the thought.

Mike made his way back to the table with their drinks.

"This place looks quite interesting, Thomas, and seems very popular," he remarked, placing the drinks on the table.

"Oh ja, most interesting, not so Heinz?"

"Ooh, Ja," squealed Heinz as his eyes lit up and he smiled knowingly at Thomas, probably for the first time that night.

"Vee get all types of people here over ze weekends," continued Thomas. "Gay, straight, bi-sexual. All flock here for some good music and fun."

"I hear the music, but what do you mean by fun?" asked Brett innocently.

Thomas laughed out loud.

"Vander about and you vill zee," said Thomas, raising his glass to the others. "I zay no more."

Out of the corner of his eye, Mike caught Heinz smirking at Thomas, his pointed little nose and tight lips almost screwed up. He wondered if Heinz was more than just an informer and if perhaps there was something between him and Thomas. Why had they arranged to meet at this club? Was Thomas gay? Or straight? Or, like Brett, bi-sexual? If he was straight, did he get some sort of satisfaction mixing with this conglomerate of people?

Thomas could see that Heinz was getting agitated by his fidgetiness and was eager to leave the company, but not before he had received his reward as an informer.

"Heinz, I shall meet you downstairs," said Thomas abruptly and forcefully. "There I vill sort you out."

Heinz's face lit up like that of a small child. He giggled, no he squeaked, loudly and hunched his shoulders, bringing his hands up to his face with joy.

"Vait for me down in ze chambers," continued Thomas, "I von't be long."

Heinz stood up, stretching his tall, slim body. He nodded and grinned to Brett and then to Mike, revealing his buck teeth, then smiled at Thomas and departed their company.

"He vishes to be paid," said Thomas, smiling at Brett and Mike, "so I shall do zat and zen he shall be happy."

"But why didn't you just slip him some money here?" asked Brett, "that's what we'd do."

Thomas laughed a deep guttural laugh.

"Oh no, not Heinz. He prefers not to get money, zen he feels zat zer is no debt. If you understand?"

Both Mike and Brett looked at each other to see if the other knew what Thomas was referring to, but both men drew a blank.

"Gentlemen," said Thomas rising and excusing himself. "Let me go and sort out Heinz. You stay and enjoy yourselves here and if you need anysing else, please do not hesitate to contact me, ja?"

"Thanks buddy," said Mike, also rising and shaking Thomas's hand. He felt the hand squeeze tightly around his own and watched the deep eyes search into his own. Again, Mike felt a stirring in his groin. What was Thomas's scene? Was he coming onto Mike?

Mike pushed this thought from his mind when Brett cut in between the two men and slapped Thomas on the back.

"Thanks for your help, Thomas. If I can ever do you a favor, let me know."

"I shall remember zat, Brett. Auf wiedesein."

The three men parted company and Brett and Mike watched as Thomas made his way downstairs. As they had finished their drinks, they decided to let the music attack their senses and also headed downstairs, where they proceeded to watch the crowds on the dance floor and at the bar counter.

The dance floor was crowded to capacity with half naked, sweaty bodies rubbing against other half naked, sweaty bodies and everyone was engrossed by the thud, thud, and thud of the music. The two men got swept up by the music and found themselves crushed against each other by the crowd as they tried to keep in time to the beat of the music on the dance floor. The air hung heavy with smoke, sweat and testosterone. For five minutes or so, Brett and Mike were lost in each other's company and the music. Suddenly the music stopped and the tempo changed.

"I don't know about you, but I think I could handle a break," said Mike, taking Brett by the arm and leading him to an open space near a flight of stairs. "At least we won't be crushed here," he said, pulling Brett close to him, almost protectively.

"Do you think that the toilets are down these steps?"

"Why, do you need to go?"

"Yep," came Brett's reply.

"Come on then. We'll never know unless we investigate, hey detective!"

The two men made their way down the winding, stone stairs. As they descended, the light diminished and they found themselves in a darkened area with a number of tunnels, almost reminiscent of the London underground, leading in various directions.

"Stay close by. I don't want to lose you," said Mike, still holding onto Brett.

"Sorry buddy, but you're never going to lose me," came the reply. "Where are we heading?"

"I don't know. I'm just following the passage and maybe we'll find a toilet."

Although it was dark, there was some light from tiny illuminations in the ceiling. They looked almost like twinkling stars sparkling among the darkness. The two men walked gingerly along a passage, feeling their way along a cold, damp wall, until they came to a small open area. Mike was leading and, as his eyes had become used to the dim lighting, he could see three outlines of people huddled together. His eyes focused on the group and from the faint light from the ceiling he could see that two of the men were busy masturbating the third. Mike stood and stared for a moment and felt his cock twitch at the sight. Brett bumped into Mike when he'd stopped.

"What have we stopped for," whispered Brett.

"Over there," whispered Mike. "In the center of the floor. Do you see?"

Brett stared until his eyes also grew accustomed to the limited light. When he saw what was happening, he squeezed Mike's arm.

"Where are we?" whispered Brett into Mike's ear.

"These must be darkrooms, or should I say more like dark dungeons," he whispered back.

They watched the threesome for a while then left them and continued along another passage. All along the wide passage were groups of men, some in pairs and others in larger groups having 'fun' as Thomas had put it.

They came to the edge of a circular area surrounded by archways leading to other passages and saw something hanging in its center. They stayed on the perimeter of the circular room, partially hidden by the darkened archways and watched. In the center, hanging from the ceiling was a sling and in it was a man with his legs raised in the air and resting on the chains, which held the sling to the ceiling. The man in the sling had long, lean legs that were spread apart and between the man's legs stood a short stocky man with his jeans down around his ankles. The man in the sling was naked and both Brett and Mike could now see that the short, stocky man had entered the thin man's ass and was fucking him with gusto. Their breathing was heavy and every time the stocky man penetrated his companion, a high-pitched squeal was emitted from the thin man.

Mike moved slightly forward into the circular area, but without either man seeing him. Brett followed and stood behind him, watching. Mike's cock was now fully erect from watching the two men fucking and he could feel his pre-cum beginning to ooze from the tip of his cock. He visualized himself in that sling with Brett fucking him. Maybe Brett was thinking the same because while Mike stood there in a trance, he felt the hardness of Brett's cock push up against his butt. He pushed back to meet Brett's thrust. Brett wrapped his arms around Mike's slim waist and pulled him closer to himself. As they stood there, totally engrossed in the display before them, Brett nibbled at the back of Mike's neck and let his hand run down Mike's chest until it came to rest on the swollen lump in the front of Mike's jeans. Brett slowly rubbed his hand up and down the length of Mike's throbbing eight inches.

Mike watched as the sling swung backwards and forwards with each thrust, with both pairs of men totally involved in their own pleasure.

"I wish I was there," whispered Mike, turning his head to meet Brett's.

"So do I," was the breathy reply. "I really want to fuck this beautiful ass of yours," said Brett, thrusting his own hardened cock up against the tightness of Mike's jeans.

The sounds coming from the pair in the sling were beginning to become louder; one deep and the other high-pitched. Mike could also see that the stocky man was increasing his thrusts both in intensity and speed. He was obviously close to coming thought Mike. Suddenly a cry came from the man in the sling and the two Englishmen saw the sling shudder violently.

"Ooh, Ja!" squealed the man in the sling as the thin man's load flew into the air and landed on his stomach and chest.

The stocky man pumped harder, holding onto his partner's hips for support. A low growl came forth from the stocky man and his body went rigid. His cock throbbed as it unloaded his seed into the belly of the thin man in the sling. When both had depleted their load and the sling had stopped swinging, the stocky man stretched across the body of his friend, without pulling out and kissed him gently on the lips. Slowly he pulled his diminishing cock from its warm environs and flicked the condom from it. He held onto his friend's legs and gently lowered them and helped the thin man from the sling. As they stood there together, arm in arm, kissing, Mike and Brett realized that it was Thomas and Heinz. So this was how Thomas repaid his informers thought Mike.

After the two Germans had left the circular area, Brett took Mike's arm and led him to the center of the area where the sling hung. Brett turned Mike around to face him and then undid his jeans for him, pulling them and his briefs down to his ankles and helping him to step out of them. As he did this, Mike pulled his T-shirt over his head and threw it onto his jeans. Mike felt the sling behind him and, holding onto the chains attached to the ceiling, lifted himself into the leather comfort of the sling and lifted his legs into the air, resting his feet on the chains, just as Heinz had done. His naked body could feel the warmth left from Heinz's body and he could also feel some stickiness from their cum. Brett stood between Mike's legs and lapped over his cock with his tongue. He made his way down to between Mike's balls and the entrance to his ass with his tongue. Both men were hard and ready for action, having watched Heinz and Thomas before them. Brett worked his way slowly towards Mike's entrance, licking as he did so until his tongue-tip reached the magic treasure cave. Mike's body twitched as Brett's tongue ran gently over his hole and their fun started.

When both men had exhausted themselves, Brett lowered Mike's legs from their vertical position and allowed them to hang over the edge of the sling while he fell across his buddy's sticky body. The two of them hugged each other as they allowed their breath to return to normality. When the two bodies were breathing as one, Brett raised his head, wiped a bead of sweat from Mike's forehead and kissed him gently on the lips. Mike reciprocated almost crushing his buddy in a bear hug.

"Wow! That was the best fuck I've ever had," whispered Mike to his friend.

"Not bad for a straight guy, hey?"

Mike burst out laughing and Brett covered his mouth with his hand to quieten him.

"You're as straight as I am," laughed Mike, "and I'm certainly no pole."

"Maybe not, but that pole between your legs sure makes up for it."

Brett helped Mike to climb from the sling and they helped each other to dress again. As they did so, another couple took their place on the sling and so life went on, just as the music did as it filtered down the tunnels from upstairs.

They went back up to the dance floor and spent some time cuddling into each other on the dance floor, this time enjoying the music as well as each other.

Returning to their hotel, they climbed into bed and again cuddled up together, knowing that their friendship was getting stronger by the day and that they were safe in each other's arms.

Chapter 10
DECISIONS

Sunday morning, Mike and Brett awoke still entangled in each other's arms. As they opened their eyes, they smiled at each other.

"Thank you for last night, Brett. I meant what I said to you last night. It really was the best."

"Why thank you for the compliment, buddy. I do try to please."

Mike felt that the bond between him and Brett was being cemented, but he was well aware that Brett was in a relationship with Belinda and he himself had feelings for Alan. He lay on his back, staring into space and thinking about what had happened this weekend.

"Brett," called Mike, "where does this put us?"

"What do you mean? We're best buddies aren't we?"

"Sure but I just wondered…" Mike broke off into deep thought. Was he taking too much for granted with Brett?

"What were you wondering?"

"What happens to us when we get back to London?"

"Life goes on, Mike. You go back to the gym and I go back to being a cop."

"And I stay on my own and you go back to Belinda!"

There was a silence from Brett.

"I see what you mean. You must understand that I love Belinda, Mike, but I also feel for you, but in a different way. You are a very special friend, and I wouldn't want to lose you, but you must understand my position as well."

"You mean a cop can't be gay or keep up a gay relationship with a man?"

"But I've been under the impression that a relationship is the last thing that you want?"

"I know what I've said in the past, but this is different, Brett."

"How's it different?"

"The fact that I let you fuck me means that you're important to me."

"Oh is that it! Do only guys who are important to you fuck you?"

"If you put it that way, I suppose so. Normally, I do the fucking."

"Well I'm sorry. I wasn't aware of that."

"Being fucked by someone that you love is very special," continued Mike, "and you're very special to me, Brett. I would hope that I wasn't just a quick screw for you last night so that you could empty those heavy balls of yours and that I meant something more to you."

"I've told you that you do, but I'm also special to Belinda. Maybe what happened last night shouldn't have happened. What about Alan? Do you have any feelings for him? What's his scene?"

Brett was becoming a little irritated by Mike's line of questioning. He was also feeling a little guilty about what had happened the previous night.

"I think we'd better get up and have breakfast and see what the day holds," said Brett getting out of the bed and heading for a shower.

Mike lay on the bed as he heard the water in the shower running. His mind kept going back to the previous evening. Both he and Brett had enjoyed their sex and Brett had been a very willing partner, but now … was Brett feeling embarrassed about the previous evening?

Brett emerged from the shower and went and sat on the bed next to Mike.

"Mike, we're the best of buddies and I don't want to lose your friendship. Having a friend is far more important than not having one and so I've given it some thought while I was in the shower; can we come to a compromise?"

Mike looked solemnly at Brett, and then answered, "What did you have in mind?"

"I know that this might sound crazy, but you really are very special to me. At the moment my mind is very confused and yes, I really did enjoy having sex with you, but I have strong feelings for Belinda. Maybe, if the urge arises, I could call on you?"

Mike looked aghast and then burst out laughing.

"You want me whenever you feel the urge or Belinda doesn't want to give it to you, is that it?" said Mike, a little peeved by Brett's suggestion.

"Not at all. It would be a two-way agreement. If you fancied a screw and you wanted me, then I'd be there for you, and vice versa. How do you feel about that?"

"How do you know you'd be there for me?" asked Mike. "What if I felt like having sex and you were busy with Belinda, would you drop her and be there for me like you say? I doubt it."

"Mike, don't make it difficult for me; you know what I mean!"

Mike thought about it. He thought about his enjoyment having Brett snugly inside of him. He thought of their friendship and how important that had been. He also thought about Belinda and Alan.

"You make it sound like a drive-in. I don't know if I want that; and what about Belinda? Is she going to have a say in this?"

"She doesn't have to know about our arrangement. As I said to you when we left for this weekend, whatever happens is between us. What do you think?"

Mike thought long and hard about this proposed arrangement. He then smiled at Brett. Brett draped his arms over Mike's shoulders and pulled him closer to him.

"I think it might take some getting used to, Brett. Then you'd be my very own fuck-buddy, so to speak!"

"It also means that you're free to date anyone you like because we're not an attachment," grinned Brett, "but be careful."

"Does it also mean that I get to fuck you occasionally?" said Mike, putting on his best innocent look.

"Now you're pushing your luck, buddy."

The two men mock-fought each other on the bed until Mike allowed Brett to dominate and sit on him.

"Does this mean that we can start from now?" asked Mike with a quizzical expression on his face, "because if it does, I can thrust my big dick up that tight ass of yours."

Brett flipped off Mike and leapt up off the bed.

"No you don't, now get dressed and let's get breakfast."

When the two friends went down for breakfast there was a message at reception for Brett.

He took the paper on which the message had been written and read: *One of the suspects has been spotted in Berlin. Contact me. Thomas.*

Brett turned to Mike and told him what Thomas had sent. While Mike went in to have breakfast, Brett put through a call to Thomas. He then went to tell Mike that they had to meet Thomas at the Tiergarten as soon as possible. They forewent breakfast and called a taxi to get them there. When they arrived they soon found Thomas waiting for them.

"I'm glad zat you could make it. Heinz phoned to tell me zat he had seen von of ze suspects here."

"Where's Heinz now?" asked Brett.

"He left ven I arrived." He pointed across the park to a large group of people. "You zee zat group, ja? Do you zee your man?"

Brett and Mike looked at the group in the distance. Brett only had Mike's description to go on.

"Do you see anyone that resembles him, Mike?"

Mike stared at the group of about forty people, sitting around some fountains, chatting or reading. His eyes went from person to person. He ignored all the females and focused his attention on the males. He noticed a few very good looking young men, but none that he recognized. Suddenly his eyes fell on an outstandingly well-built man in a tight white T-shirt that revealed heavy pecs, massive biceps and a slim, trim waist. Mike was silent as his eyes made contact with those of the hunk. There was an almost pained look in the eyes of the hunk as he stared back at Mike.

"Do you see anything," repeated Brett, a little agitatedly.

Mike was mesmerized by the rugged beauty of the hunk, but what was this man doing here in Berlin, of all cities. Why was it that wherever Mike was, the hunk seemed to be?

Brett repeated his questioning of Mike. "Do you see anything?"

Mike turned to Brett and quietly said, "He's there."

"Where?" asked Brett, eagerly.

"There," said Mike turning back to face the hunk's eyes; but when he did so, he couldn't see him. "He was there," shouted Mike, pointing in the direction of the fountain. "I saw him."

"He can't have vanished. Come, let's get there and check," said Brett starting to run towards the group, with Mike and Thomas in tow.

When all three reached the group, Brett and Thomas started asking the remaining people around the fountain area if they knew where the muscular man had gone. Most of them looked surprised at the questioning and chose to ignore Brett and Thomas.

"What man?" queried some of them, indignantly.

Even after Thomas told them he was connected to the police, they still took little notice of the three of them. While Brett and Thomas continued to try to get information from the people, Mike tended to stand aside, deep in thought. Why was this man following him and who was he? Then he saw a red 4 X 4 drive slowly past with the hunk at the wheel. Once again their eyes met and searched into each other's soul. Mike stood there watching as the vehicle faded into the distance.

Eventually, Brett and Thomas, having got no information that could be of use to them from the rest of the group, together with Mike, went back to the hotel, without Mike making mention of the 4 X 4.

Back at the hotel, they went up to Mike and Brett's room and ordered something to drink.

"I can't understand how he could have vanished like that, so suddenly," commented Brett. "Are you sure that it was him, Mike?"

Mike never responded.

"You're very quiet, Mike. Are you okay?"

"Sure, Brett, it's nothing much. Just thinking of this guy and why he seems to be following me."

"According to Heinz," interrupted Thomas, "zis is definitely von of zee robbers, zis bodybuilder."

"But why is he haunting me? What is the connection between him, me and the robbery?" bemoaned Mike.

"If we knew that, we wouldn't have all these problems. Just chill, buddy," said Brett putting an arm around Mike's shoulders to console him. "Look at it in a positive light, the guy isn't stalking you with the intent to do you bodily harm."

"How do you know?"

"Well, I'm sure that he wouldn't have waited this long before doing something."

"With a body like his, I wouldn't mind if he did me bodily harm," joked Mike.

With this last comment, the solemn atmosphere broke and the three men started to laugh together.

"I'm glad to see that you haven't lost your sense of humor," grinned Brett.

Brett then turned to Thomas.

"By the way, Thomas, to change the subject just a little, thank you for last night," said Brett with a glint in his eye as he said so.

"Did you enjoy yourselves?" asked Thomas politely, "and did you behave yourselves?"

"If it weren't for you, we probably would have behaved ourselves," answered Mike, "but we followed your example."

Thomas looked a little puzzled by this statement.

"I do not understand?"

Mike and Brett looked at each other, and then from grinning faces they told Thomas about seeing him and Heinz the previous evening and how their action had turned them on and what had happened between the two Englishmen.

Thomas smiled almost beatifically as though he blessed their lovemaking and approved of it.

"If you are in Germany, you must love like a German," he said. "Be passionate and enjoy vot you do vith each other. Make it special so zat it is a lasting moment, not somezing to be embarrassed about. Love each other and give zanks for each other, because vee never know when vee vill lose ze one zat vee love, ja?"

Mike and Brett smiled to each other and Mike held out his hand for Brett to hold.

"I think I know what you mean Thomas. Brett and I come from different backgrounds, but we are being brought closer together and I don't think that anything will come between our friendships, do you Brett?"

Brett squeezed Mike's hand and as he did so, Mike was sure that he saw some tears beginning to well up in Brett's eyes.

"Love is very special," continued Thomas. "Ven you have someone to love, you must verk on it and not let it happen on its own. Just like a musician must practice his musical skills, so must a lover. Just as you must feed a child, so you must feed each other vith love."

"Do you have someone that you love, Thomas," asked Brett.

"I did, but he died," he replied sadly. "Perhaps I loved him too much."

"We're sorry to hear that," said the two men. "Were you together for a long time?" asked Mike.

"Six years, then he had an accident. Zince then I have had no von in my life."

"But you enjoy life?" asked Mike.

"Oh ja, too much. Zat is why I come out whenever I can and enjoy myself. Life is to be lived or you just die, ja?"

The two men agreed with him.

The three, as they had become friends, spent the rest of the day together until it was time for them to make their way to the airport for the return journey. Thomas drove them to the airport, chatting all the way and inviting them either together or separately to come back and spend some time in Berlin with him.

"Next time I show you even better places to visit."

"What could be better than where you took us last night?"

Thomas laughed and nudged Brett.

"I show you much better place next time, maybe I take you to sauna where ze heat arouses you and ze bodies are sweaty and smooth, ja?"

"Only if I'm allowed to come with Brett," joked Mike.

The three bade their farewells at the airport and soon Brett and Mike were winging their way back to London. When they landed, Brett turned to Mike and said, "Remember, not a word to Belinda."

As they moved through the arrivals hall and the customs and exited to the multitudes waiting to be greeted by family and friends, Mike froze. Standing amongst the greeting people was his muscular hunk.

Chapter 11
SWEET DREAMS

On the Monday, back at the gym, Mike phoned Alan to say that he was back and what had happened in Berlin – well not quite everything that happened. He kept his liaison with Brett to himself and never gave any indication to Alan of where they had been or what they did, other than aspects related to their investigation, even though Alan did enquire. He felt that the less Alan know of the tryst with Brett, the better, just in case Alan misunderstood the situation, because after all, Mike did have feelings for Alan, but at this moment in time, Mike's mind was befuddled.

Alan came round to the gym later in the afternoon for a workout, after which he and Mike spent some time chatting together in the refreshment area. Mike told him about seeing the hunk at the Tiergarten and then again at Heathrow Airport when they returned.

"Why do you think he also went to Berlin?" asked Alan.

"Beats me, but what beats me even more was the fact that as we came through customs, I saw him standing amongst the crowds at arrivals."

"Mike, are you sure that it was him that you saw and that you didn't see a double, because I think this thing is actually getting to you?"

"Alan, I know what I saw. But it is spooking me a little."

"But if he's after you for some reason, why did he appear to me in the showers?"

"You're right. I just don't understand what's going on."

"Mike, have you spoken to anyone else other than Brett and me?"

"Not a soul knows." He hesitated to think and then added, "Sorry, Steven also knows. I mean he knows about the hunk being in the shower area, but he knows nothing about any sexual activities; I wouldn't dare tell him. I don't of course know whether he's told anyone about these events, but I doubt it."

Mike and Alan spent about another half hour together and then Alan left to go home. However, before he left, he asked Mike if he wanted to come round and have a drink with him after work. Mike decided that after his hectic weekend in Berlin, all he wanted was to have an early night at home, so the offer was turned down. Before he left, Mike phoned Brett to find out if he'd heard anything more about their investigation.

"I haven't heard any more from Thomas, but I'm sure that if he gets any news, we'll be the first to hear."

"Did Belinda ask you about the weekend?"

"She just wanted to know whether we had any luck and I told her of our meeting with Thomas and Heinz."

"And about us?"

"She asked if we'd had a good time."

"I sincerely hope you said YES!" Mike exclaimed, shouting out the word 'yes'.

"No I just told her that we hadn't much time to do anything except meet with Thomas, and that we had seen quite a bit of the inside of the hotel."

"That's no lie. Do you think she might be suspicious?"

"No, not at all. I wouldn't worry, buddy. It's our little secret and it will remain like that. Have you said anything to Alan?"

"Do you mean about us?"

"Hm."

"Not a word, because I don't know how he would take it."

"Good, keep it like that," retorted Brett.

Mike promised to phone Brett the following day and then hung up. The remainder of the afternoon was spent training some of his clients, taking a well-earned shower at the end of his work day and then heading for home.

When he arrived at his apartment, he put on some music and started to prepare dinner for himself. While the vegetables bubbled away on the stove, Mike went into his bedroom and stripped off. Now that he was alone at home and it was still warm, he chose to wander around his home naked.

His dinner was put into the oven and then he poured himself a drink and sprawled out on his couch, listening to the cool sounds of some jazz. What a pleasure from the heavy metal that Alan had played to him, he thought. As he lay there, his mind went back to Berlin and the evening with Brett. It had made an enormous impact on him.

At first he thought it was because of the novelty of a 'straight' guy having had sex with him, but then the more he thought of Brett, the more he began to think that in fact there was a strong bond, both mentally and sexually, between them. He then thought about Alan. How did he compare with Brett? No, this wasn't a beauty competition where you had to choose a winner. Both men had different qualities and both appealed to him. Alan had simplicity and a youthful innocence about him and Mike felt he needed to protect him, whereas he wanted to be protected by Brett. He felt secure and safe in Brett's arms. His emotions were in turmoil but he was not prepared to play one off against the other. He knew that Brett had strong feelings for Belinda, and Mike liked her very much. What he found disturbing within the turmoil in his mind: he wanted to love someone and have a relationship with that person, but at the moment, there were two people in his life who meant so much to him.

On the one mental level his head was saying that Alan would be the ideal person, yet his heart was longing for Brett. On a physical level, he found both men incredibly sexy and beautiful in bed.

The timer in the kitchen sounded and brought Mike back to the reality of home living. He went into the kitchen and switched the stove off and dished up his dinner. How awful to have to cook for one, he thought. How much nicer it would be to cook for someone else or maybe two others.

Mike made his way back into the lounge, turned off his hi-fi and switched on the TV. The news was on, but he didn't take much interest in what he called depressing, morbid crap.

However, he chose not to switch the TV set off. He tucked into his meal, channel-hopped on the TV for a while, and when he'd finished eating, went back to the kitchen and placed his dirty plate in the sink. He was tired so he decided to call it a day and wandered off to his bedroom, switching off the TV and the lounge lights. Without switching on the bedroom light, Mike collapsed onto his bed, slid under the duvet and started to doze off to the land of dreams.

Mike fell quickly to sleep, a deep sleep that his body obviously needed. It must have been after a few hours that he began to dream. He shifted his position on the bed and kicked off his duvet so that his body was completely exposed to the warm night air.

He saw his muscular hunk standing at the bottom of the bed, as he'd seen him in Berlin with the white, tight T-shirt and the bulging muscles. He stood at the foot of the bed with his hands splayed across the front of his equally tight jeans that revealed the tell-tale bulge in the front. Mike's hand slid unconsciously down to his crotch and scooped up his balls and gently squeezed them. Again, he restlessly adjusted his sleeping position on the bed.

The hunk at the foot of the bed slowly began to remove his shirt and Mike could see his arm and shoulder muscles move in perfect synchronicity as he did so. As he pulled the T-shirt over his head, stretching his arms and puffing out his chest, his tapered waist and tight abs came into view. He flung the T-shirt onto the floor and then very seductively unzipped his jeans. Placing his hand on the waistband of his jeans, he slowly pushed them down over his hips, revealing a huge bulge enclosed within his white HOM briefs. The jeans fell to the floor and the hunk stepped out of them. He then lowered himself onto the bed and positioned himself next to Mike. Again, Mike adjusted his position on the bed, this time lying flat on his back.

Mike heard the hunk say, "Do you want me?"

Mike groaned in his sleep.

"I know you want me. From the first time you saw me you wanted me," whispered the man.

Again Mike groaned.

"I want to fuck you, just as you want to be fucked by me," continued the whisper.

Once more Mike groaned, but this time with a little more enthusiasm.

The hunk moved closer to Mike and slid his muscular body on top of Mike's, rubbing his chest over Mike's so that their raised nipples came into contact, then he maneuvered his swelling cock over Mike's equally swelling cock. As the two cocks rubbed against each other, Mike thrust his hips into the air and continued to groan. This continued for a minute or two, and then the hunk pulled down his HOM briefs revealing his long shaft with a swollen mushroom-shaped head. Some pre-cum oozed from the piss-slip of the hunk. As their cocks rubbed together, so his pre-cum lubricated the two cock-heads, one circumcised and the other not.

As flesh glided over flesh, Mike's body thrashed on the bed. The guy moved to between Mike's legs and gently parted them with his hands, allowing himself access to Mike's heavy balls and soft silky pubes.

Mike felt the warm hands cup his balls and gently squeeze them, and then he felt those same hands wrap around his length and start to massage his cock. His groaning increased in amplitude, as did his breathing. The hunk rolled Mike onto his stomach and positioning his cock near Mike's anus, proceeded to slide his bargepole over the crack created by Mike's firm ass. Again Mike pushed his ass upwards, inviting the hunk to take him. The hunk continued to rub up and down the crack between Mike's ass cheeks, resting on his elbows as he did so. His biceps flexed as he took his weight off of Mike's body and let only his cock touch Mike.

After some time, he leaned across Mike and took a condom from the side table next to the bed, sat up astride Mike's prone body and seductively unrolled it over his cock, squeezing his cock as he did so. So large was his erection that the condom never reached down to the base of his cock, but he admired his length and girth, that was rock hard, that lay in his hand. His manhood flexed and he repositioned himself above Mike aiming his weapon at Mike's twitching asshole. With both hands, he held Mike's ass cheeks apart and admired the small pink rose that was quivering like a heartbeat in anticipation. When the head of his cock touched Mike's waiting entrance, it was as though some suction was in force as his rose bud opened like a flower in bloom and dragged the hunk's cock into his depths.

He groaned as he saw his cock slowly disappear into the warmth of Mike. His push was slow and gentle, not wanting to hurt, but rather give pleasure. When he had gone in about three inches, he stopped to allow Mike's ass muscles to relax around this giant weapon. The whole time he watched that small pink bud open and clamp around his stem. When he felt ready, he continued his slow journey to the land of milk and honey: ecstasy.

The hunk watched as he sank his cock to the very depths of Mike's bowels and felt his balls rest against Mike's butt. He held his position for a while, luxuriating in the inner warmth and protection that his cock enjoyed, and then he began a slow withdrawal. He felt the pink rosebud clamp even tighter, as if to say 'don't go'. He pulled back until he saw that the lip of his mushroom-headed cock was about to break through the sphincter muscle, then he once again slowly sank his shaft back down into that warm depth.

A slow rhythmic fuck began with Mike's upward thrusts coinciding with his deep groans. The hunk's deep penetrations became more intense as he built up momentum. He used his strong muscular arms as support so that he could watch his cock grinding into Mike's tight ass. This continued for some time, with the man's actions becoming more frenetic with each thrust into Mike's body. The hunk's body gleamed with sweat and this made sliding over Mike's body more sensual. Mike could hear the slapping of flesh against flesh as one muscular man pounded into the other's muscular body. It was muscle against muscle, cock against ass and pleasure against pain.

Although Mike's firm ass had accepted the hunk, his deep penetrations brought a painful pleasure to Mike. Mike could feel his prostate being pounded and this was bringing him closer and closer to the edge of his climax.

A loud gasp echoed around the silence of the room as Mike fired his load into the sheets. His muscles tightened and the grip on the hunk's cock became intense. He felt the hunk's bargepole throb and jerk as it shot a load into the tip of the condom. Every muscle in the hunk's body flexed as he pushed further into Mike as the second shot left his piss-slit, and for the next five shots, he dug deep into the realms of Mike's squirming ass, perspiration coating his gleaming body. The wetness of the man's body added to the sensuality of the occasion, sliding his glowing chest over Mike's back muscles.

When the hunk was depleted of warm cum and could feel it coating his sheathed dick, he lowered his body onto that of Mike's and wrapped his arms around him. "I wanted you," he whispered into Mike's ear, but Mike was still in dreamland.

"Who are you?" mumbled Mike in his sleep.

"Bruno," whispered the hunk into Mike's ear, "and I need to speak to you."

A shrill ringing sound woke Mike as his alarm clock hit its deadline and began to perform. He opened his eyes and stretched out an arm and hit the clock, cutting off the invasive sound. He lay there for a while allowing his eyes to get used to the daylight now streaming through the bedroom windows, then rolled over onto his back, yawned and slid his hand down between his legs and felt his hard-on. A smile formed on his mouth and he rubbed his length, forcing his foreskin to roll back to reveal his pink cock head.

"Hmm," he sighed, playing with his hard-on and pulling at his foreskin, "that was a great night's sleep." He cupped his balls and gave them a wake-up squeeze then he stretched his whole body; his arms moved across the bed and he felt the wetness of the sheet beneath him.

"Oh fuck, a bloody wet dream," he cursed. "I thought I was past that stage," he muttered to himself.

He got up from the bed and pulled the bottom sheet from the mattress. As he did so something fell to the floor. He went around to the other side of the bed and picked up the object. It was a white pair of HOM briefs and on the side table next to the bed was a used condom.

Chapter 12
THAT'S WHAT FRIENDS ARE FOR

Panic struck Mike. Had he dreamed this fantastic experience the night before or was it real, and if it was real, which he believed it to be, how did the hunk manage to enter his apartment? Was he losing it? Was his mind playing tricks on him? He picked up the HOM briefs and held them to his nose. He inhaled deeply and closed his eyes as he did so. The manly odors of the hunk filtered up through his nostrils. He could smell the sickly sweet sweat, deodorant and traces of urine, which sent his mind into a euphoric state. He held the briefs there for some time, breathing deeply. He then picked up the used condom and studied the contents. It struck him just how much there was in the condom; obviously its owner had contained a great quantity that needed to be freed. He sat on the edge of his bed, with briefs in one hand and condom in the other while thoughts flashed through his mind. Who? What? When? How? And why?

Still sitting on the bed, his next decision was to phone someone, but was it to be Brett or Alan? His contact with Alan was more recent than that with Brett but Brett had been to Berlin with him and after all, he was a cop. He needed reassurance and although he knew both men would give it to him; he finally decided to phone Brett.

He moved into the toilet and flushed the used condom away, then went into the lounge, sat down on his couch, lifted his legs and placed them on his piece de resistance, his solid marble coffee table, and dialed Brett's home number. The phone rang for some time before it was answered. While he sat there waiting, he could feel the coldness of the marble against the backs of his legs. The phone was answered and the voice on the other end was Belinda's. On hearing her voice he realized that she had obviously spent the night with Brett. He also knew that if they had spent the night together, they would probably have had sex together. He envied Belinda having Brett make love to her and he wished that at this exact moment, Brett had been making love to him.

"Hi Belinda. Sorry to trouble you, but is Brett there?" His voice trembled as he spoke to her, not because he feared her in any way, but it was dawning on him that his privacy, his whole being had been invaded by some stranger, if it were real.

"What's the matter Mike? You sound upset about something?" said Belinda.

"Is he there, please?"

He didn't want to start explaining to her what had happened. He just wanted Brett to be with him.

Brett came onto the phone.

"Hi buddy, what's the problem?"

Tears began to fill Mike's eyes when he heard Brett's voice.

"Please come over here, I need to see you?"

"What's happened, Mike? You really sound upset."

"Please just get here. I'll explain when you get here."

Mike couldn't speak any more for fear that he would burst into tears, so he put the phone down. It was at this moment that he realized that he wasn't sure whether he was on the brink of a nervous breakdown.

Mike sat in the lounge waiting for Brett to arrive, trying to fathom out the previous night's events. While he sat there, his phone rang. He jumped with fright, then he raised his head and looked at it. He hesitated before deciding to answer. Maybe it was Brett.

"Hello, Mike Schwantz speaking," he said in a solemn, subdued tone.

"Hi Mike, it's Alan," came the sprightly voice on the other end of the line. "I just phoned to say good morning and find out how you are."

This was not what Mike wanted. It was not that he didn't want to speak to Alan, but he had enough problems of his own without lumbering them onto Alan. Mike fought back the tears once more in an effort to control his emotions.

"Hi Alan, I'm fine thanks."

The answer was brief and curt. This was not the Mike that Alan or anyone else knew. Mike was the outgoing, gregarious type of man who enjoyed life to the full, not this insecure sounding person on the other end of the telephone line.

"Hey, what's the matter?" enquired Alan, with concern in his voice. "What's happened?"

Mike didn't know whether to mention anything to Alan, but he felt that discretion was better. He didn't answer. There was a deathly hush on the line.

"Mike! Are you there?"

"Yes, I'm here," was the soft reply.

"Something's happened, hasn't it?"

Mike knew that he really couldn't keep things from Alan because he was becoming part of Mike's life and couldn't keep secrets from him.

In a tear-choking voice, he replied, "Yes."

"You stay put, buddy. I'm coming around to your place. Don't do anything or go anywhere. I'll be there within the next half an hour."

Mike had never heard Alan so assertive. Here was this nineteen-year old showing control and from the tone of his voice, Mike felt a little more secure in the knowledge that he had friends on whom he could rely.

He heard the phone go 'click' and the line go dead. Alan was already on his way.

Mike went into the kitchen, made a cup of tea and went back into the lounge to wait.

True to his word, within half an hour, the front doorbell rang. Mike opened it and there stood Alan. He flung his arms around Mike's neck and hugged him in the doorway.

"What's the problem, buddy?"

At that point Mike broke down. The pent-up tension and emotions just burst forth. Mike sobbed and sobbed into Alan's neck, and all the while Alan tried to pacify him. They stood there for what must have felt like an eternity before Alan actually crossed the threshold into Mike's apartment and closed the front door.

Alan led Mike to the lounge and they seated themselves on the couch together. Mike could see the concern in Alan's eyes, but he thought it selfish to burden his young friend with his woes. Alan took hold of Mike's hands and, holding them tightly in his own, looked him squarely in the eyes.

"Now speak to me. I care very much for you, you know that, so don't give me any crap, do you understand! What's happened?"

Mike, now having managed to keep his emotions under control, picked up the white pair of HOM briefs that now lay of the coffee table in front of them. He held them up to show Alan. Alan looked at them and then at Mike.

"So? What are you showing me your underwear for?"

Mike's voice floated from somewhere deep inside of him.

"They're not mine, Alan," he said in a breathy tone.

Alan couldn't help the laugh that emitted from him.

"You mean that this is all about a pair of briefs! Whose are they then, because they don't look like mine?"

"I wish they were yours," remarked Mike, meaning every word that he said. "No these I found in the bed this morning."

Alan's voice dropped to a concerned whisper. With a tone of disappointment in his voice, he asked, "Did you have someone in your bed last night?"

Mike realized that if he said 'yes' it was going to hurt Alan's feelings, because Alan might construe it as that he only slept with Alan when he wanted a fuck and that there were no emotional attachments involved.

"I don't know," came the awkward reply.

"What do you mean you don't know, here's the evidence," replied Alan, holding the white pair of briefs.

Mike had to clear up any misunderstanding between the two of them so he proceeded to tell Alan of the whole night's events.

"There, I've told you everything that happened," said Mike with a certain relief in his voice, "and this is why I'm confused. I keep thinking it's all a dream, but these briefs and a used condom are not figments of the imagination! I didn't want to bring you into my problems, and that's why I didn't want to say anything in the beginning. I didn't want you to misunderstand. I've realized that you mean a great deal to me and I didn't want you to worry, that's all."

Alan held Mike in his arms and the two hugged each other. They were still in that position when the doorbell rang again.

"That'll be Brett," said Mike, crossing to the front door and opening it for his other friend.

Brett came in and saw Alan sitting in the lounge.

"Hi Alan, I'm glad that you got round here for our buddy."

Alan greeted Brett and then shifted along the couch so that all three were able to sit together, Mike seated in the middle.

Mike once again repeated the whole night's events to Brett and showed him the evidence. Brett listened intently, then rose and began to look around the room.

"What are you looking for?" enquired Mike.

"I wanted to see if there was any break-in. How did he get into your apartment?"

None of the windows had been forced, neither had the front door. In fact there was no sign anywhere in the apartment of a forced entry.

Brett sat down again and looked at Mike.

"You know Mike, there is no way that guy forced his way into your home. Please don't misunderstand what I'm about to say, but the only way in which he could have gained entry is by the front door being opened."

"Are you suggesting that I willingly invited him into my home?"

"It could appear like that. I emphasise, could."

Mike looked at both Brett and Alan for reassurance.

"I didn't, I promise," he wailed.

This new suggestion did plant a seed of doubt in his mind. Yes, he had found the hunk extremely attractive in a lustful way, but had never mentioned this to anyone, and wouldn't do so now. Yes, he had enjoyed their fleeting moment in the shower at the gym, but no, he hadn't invited him into his home.

"If I had invited him in, as you might be suggesting, surely I would have known what I was doing last night and wouldn't have phoned you to tell you what I'd found?"

Alan came to the rescue.

"He does have a point there, Brett."

"Okay," agreed Brett, "let's forget about how he got in. Think back to last night. Do you remember in your 'dream' as you put it, anything else, other than the actual sex?"

Mike sat thinking, trying desperately to be of assistance to his friends.

"Was it purely a visual dream? What I mean is that sometimes when we dream, we only see the visuals and there is no sound, but at other times we feel as though we are speaking in our dreams. Haven't you heard people talking in their sleep? Well, was there anything like that?"

Again Mike was silent as he tried to dig deep into the depths of his subconscious. He searched Alan's face for help, then Brett's, but he couldn't remember anything.

"No," came the feeble answer.

There was an awkward silence as the three sat on the couch together.

Mike's mind suddenly flashed. He did remember something, vaguely. Somewhere in his mind he could hear the words, 'you want me' and 'I want to fuck you, just as you want to be fucked by me.' These words were now spinning around his head. Had someone actually said this to him or was this autosuggestion. Was he merely wishing these thoughts? He looked at his two friends again. He loved them both in different ways, but to his hunk he merely lusted for his strong masculine body. He wanted to be controlled and dominated by this hunk, but he didn't feel the need for the same domination from either Brett or Alan. They would never understand this inner dilemma that he faced. Perhaps he felt that he wanted to have all the physical attributes that his hunk had, but he did in fact have them. He was good looking, well-built, a charming personality, a tight ass and was well hung; all the attributes that Brett and Alan enjoyed. Or, was it that he just wanted to be dominated, period?

"I'm still trying to think," came Mike's feeble voice.

"Well I can't sit here all day," said Brett, "some of us have to go to work, or aren't you two going to work today?"

"I'm going to phone in sick today," said Mike. "I need to take control of this situation and sort myself out."

"If it's okay with you, Mike, could I spend some of this day with you and help you 'sort things out'?" asked Alan.

"That would be nice. I'd like that," and for the first time that morning, Mike flashed a smile.

Brett and Alan stood up and Brett gave Alan a spontaneous hug.

"Keep an eye on him, buddy, he's very special to both of us."

Alan looked deeply into Brett's eyes and saw a glint of something.

"I think I know what you mean," came his reply. "Yes he's very special."

Alan turned to Mike.

"Don't worry, I'll see Brett to the door," and with that, Mike's two buddies left the lounge.

Mike heard the front door open and the lowered voices of Brett and Alan at the front entrance.

Suddenly he leapt from his seat on the couch and rushed to the front door.

"Bruno!" he shouted.

Alan and Brett both stood shocked by this sudden outburst.

"The name Bruno keeps flashing through my mind. I'm sure that somewhere that name was raised, but I could be wrong."

It was the first time that both Brett and Alan saw a glimmer of relief in Mike's face.

"Bruno? Right," said Brett, "I'll try that name, but in the meantime, if you two guys are not going to work and you do go out, please take your mobile phone with you in case I need to get in touch, okay?"

With that, Brett departed, leaving Alan and Mike to spend the day together.

Chapter 13
REVELATION

"What do you feel like doing today, Mike?" asked Alan, heading to the kitchen to make them both some tea.

"I really haven't given it much thought, but I'd better first phone work."

"I wouldn't tell Steven the real reason why you're not going in to work, even if he does ask. I don't know, but there's something that I just don't like about that guy."

"Ah, he's pretty harmless, I think," replied Mike as be began to dial the gym's telephone number.

When he got through, Steven wasn't there yet, so Mike left a message to say that he wouldn't be at work, as he wasn't feeling well, and left it at that. In the meantime, Alan had made tea for them and taken it through to the lounge.

"You're becoming quite part of the furniture aren't you? But I'm glad," commented Mike.

"Hey I'm here to help you and that's what buddies are for, aren't they?"

"Sometimes I think they're worth more than just a help, and I know that you mean a great deal more to me, Alan, and I appreciate you being who you are and what you do for me."

Alan blushed as Mike passed these compliments.

"You're embarrassing me."

"Please, you don't get embarrassed," joked Mike, giving his buddy a friendly punch on the arm, "I mean it."

"Aargh!" cried Alan, flinching in mock pain. "You've mortally wounded me."

He fell back onto the couch, pretending to have been knocked out.

"Now what am I going to do?" sighed Mike, pretending to be concerned.

"You could give me mouth to mouth resuscitation", came a little voice from the prone figure on the couch.

Both men burst out laughing and lay hugging and kissing each other on the couch.

"Alan, you really are a true friend and I think I really do love you," said Mike, breaking away from Alan's kisses and looking dreamily into his eyes. "I know that you're good for me, but there are still some issues that I need to sort out."

"And I think I love you too," answered Alan, giving Mike a peck on the nose. "But don't worry, we'll work through those issues together, if you'd like."

Mike leapt up from the couch and turned to Alan.

"Do you know what I want to do?"

"I might have an idea," replied Alan, smiling mischievously at Mike.

"Let's spend the day doing nothing around London."

"Well, to be honest, that's not what I had in mind."

"And pray good sir, what did you have in mind, you horny little devil?"

"Let's make love! But let's do it all day."

"Do you think you've got the staying power to keep up with me?" teased Mike.

"You'll never know unless you try."

Mike pulled Alan close to him and gave him a great bear hug.

"What am I going to do with you?"

"You could have a serious relationship with me, or you could do worse."

The words suddenly struck Mike. He stared at Alan and then he fell silent as they sank in. No one had ever asked him to have a relationship; it had always been him to make the first move. He had always found that people only wanted him for his body and here was a beautiful young man who wanted more than just that. He stared into Alan's eyes, which seemed to get softer in the light. Very quietly he said, "I think I'd like that very much."

They stood there for at least eight or nine minutes, cuddling each other but neither saying a word. There was just the silence of the apartment and the warmth generated between the two men, yet the atmosphere felt electric.

They eventually set off for their day around London, both with a spring in their step as they made their way to the underground. They first headed off to Piccadilly Circus because Alan wanted to go to Virgin Records to get some CDs. Mike quickly realised that if they were to have a meaningful relationship he would have to learn to appreciate Alan's interests more and this meant getting to know and perhaps like heavy metal music. It was not to say that Mike didn't enjoy music, because he did, and he enjoyed scratching through the CDs looking for music for Alan and himself.

"What do you think of him?" asked Alan, holding up a CD by George Michael.

"Do you mean his singing or his looks?"

"Both," replied Alan. "Don't you find him sexy?"

Mike took the CD and looked at the cover photograph. He studied it for a while and then handed it back to Alan, shaking his head.

"I think you're sexier."

"No, but serious, what do you think of him? Would you like to bed him?"

"Why are you asking me these strange questions?"

"Because I want to know more about you and what your likes and dislikes are."

Mike studied Alan's expectant face.

"I suppose I wouldn't mind spending a night in bed with him."

"That makes two of us," said Alan excitedly. "There, you see we already have something in common."

Mike laughed and tousled Alan's hair. "You're incorrigible."

But Alan was not stopping there.

"Can you just imagine the three of us in bed together?" he said, looking dreamily at the photo on the CD.

Mike smiled at him.

"Yes, actually I can. You humping George Michael while I lie in bed reading a book."

"Why won't you take me seriously?" asked Alan.

"Would you really like that, a threesome? And who's doing whom? Have you worked out that equation yet?"

Alan thought for a while then he said, "We can take turns."

"What do you mean take turns? You make it sound like a merry-go-round."

"Well you could have him, then he could have me and then you could have me…"

"… And who has me?"

Alan grinned like a Cheshire cat. It was as though Mike's comment had been scripted specially for him.

"Brett!" answered Alan in a hushed tone. "Would you like that?"

Mike could feel the blood rush to both his face. The idea was indeed pleasing to him, with or without George Michael. To eliminate his embarrassment, he merely laughed and said, "Where did that idea originate from?"

Alan's smile dissipated a little and taking Mike's arm, he said, "I know that this is one of your issues that you said you needed to sort out, but it can be sorted out very easily."

"Oh and have you got it all planned out?"

"Before Brett left your apartment this morning, he mentioned something to me about Berlin. He was brief and didn't have time to fill in all the details, but I know where you're coming from and I know that you have your desires as well. For me, I know what I want. I want you to make love to me, to be a part of me and for me to be a part of you. I enjoy being with you and having you inside of me and possessing me. I enjoy pleasing you sexually and that turns me on, but I don't have a desire to fuck anybody. With you it's different. I hope that I satisfy you mentally and sexually and that you want to make love to me, but I also now know that you too want to be possessed, to be dominated. I can care for you in that sense, but I can't possess you sexually and I know that you have very strong feelings for Brett."

"So where is this all leading?" interrupted Mike.

"I want you to know that if you feel that way for Brett, it's okay with me - provided you're not screwing him, added Alan."

Mike was dumbstruck. He fell silent and just looked into Alan's open face. The young man showed understanding beyond his years and he meant every word he had spoken. It was as though everything that Mike had desired was beginning to fall into place; someone to care for and love and someone to dominate and possess him sexually.

"Alan told me that you had sex with each other and that he'd screwed you. Is that true?"

Mike looked sheepishly at Alan, then, putting his arms around his waist, he said, "Yes that's true. I can't lie to you".

"And did you enjoy it?"

After some hesitation, Mike responded. "Yes, it was the most immense feeling, but a totally different feeling from when I make love to you. When a guy fucks me I succumb to his masculinity and strength and to me it's a full-on turn on, but if you're prepared to forgive me for what I did…"

"…all you did was have someone dominate you sexually. Now perhaps you'll understand the pleasure that you give me when you dominate my body."

"What can I say?" were the only words that a bewildered Mike could say.

"How about thanks?"

Mike pulled Alan closer to him and placed his lips gently on Alan's and both maintained an enduring kiss.

"But tell me, what about his girlfriend? Does she know and approve?"

"No! Definitely not. She doesn't know. That was the condition; we were not to say anything to her."

"But then what's his scene?" enquired Alan.

"He's bi-sexual."

Although there was still the mystery of the hunk, Mike felt that a load had been shifted from his shoulders.

"So where do we go from here?" he asked Alan.

"To the London Eye," said Alan, excitedly, brushing the whole incident away.

High up on the wheel, they surveyed the beauty of the London skyline. They excitedly looked for landmarks and took pleasure in each other's company. They were like two small children on their first outing to the big city. They moved from one side of the cabin to the other, looking through the vast windows at the magnificence of the busy city. Down on the muddy river, boats toiled, and adjacent to the Thames they could see the businessmen and tourists going about their daily business. High above the city, it seemed that they were closer to heaven, literally and metaphorically speaking.

Slowly their cabin began its descent. They continued to find buildings and objects that they had missed on their way up in the cabin. Down below them, the people were like ants, insignificant and small, yet busily moving around, but among this crowd there was one who stood out from the rest. Mike nudged Alan. Alan could see the alarmed look on Mike's face. He looked down but was unaware of what Mike was looking at.

"What's the matter?" he asked, still searching for the cause of Mike's alarmed reaction.

"Down there. It's him," he whispered in disbelief, pointing to a group of people below the wheel.

Alan strained his eyes to find the person, until Mike pointed the direction in which to look.

There below them majestically stood the hunk, hands on hips, legs astride and looking up at the wheel. Mike felt an adrenalin rush and a surge in his groin. Was this the man who had brought him pleasure last night? If it was, why did he leave his briefs and his filled condom? Were these reminders of his virility or just mementoes for Mike to keep?

Alan moved closer to Mike, almost as if to protect him.

"It's okay, Mike. Don't worry about a thing."

As the wheel turned and they neared the disembarking area, Mike noticed that for the first time ever, when their eyes met, the hunk smiled at him, then turned and walked away. Alan noticed this as well. Mike could feel his groin aching from the memories of the previous night. His cock flinched and his ass muscles clamped his butt cheeks together, like they had done last night. Alan noticed Mike's reaction and felt a reaction of his own. He too had been confronted by the hunk and was taken by his physical prowess. Alan could also feel his cock jolt into life and tried surreptitiously to adjust his rising erection. Mike noticed Alan's actions and smiled at him.

"You too, hey buddy?"

"Yep, me too," was his brief response as he pushed his hand into the front of his jeans and openly adjusted the lie of his rapidly swelling cock.

Chapter 14
A VISITOR

Mike and Alan spent the morning together and then enjoyed each other's company over a pub lunch. Mike had said that he wanted to go back to his apartment and have a sleep in the afternoon and that if Alan wanted to join him he was more than welcome. Alan said that he wanted to do some more shopping so he'd stay in the city and then go round to Mike's apartment that evening.

"Why not bring some clothes and spend the night, then in the morning you can go to work from there," suggested Mike.

"That sounds like a great idea, but will you be fine for the rest of the day?"

"Sure, don't you worry about a thing, I'll be fine. Oh and one other thing," he said, lowering his voice, "don't let anyone attack that cute ass of yours. That now belongs to me." Mike gave Alan's cute ass a squeeze, feeling its firmness.

"Hmm! That feels ripe and ready to pluck," he said, kissing Alan on the cheek and not worrying whether passers-by saw.

He got back to his apartment, climbed onto the bed and was just dozing off to sleep when his mobile phone rang. It was Brett.

"Hi buddy, how's today been?"

"Hi Brett. It's been just great. I've got so much to tell you…"

"…I'm sure you have. Is Alan with you?"

"No he wanted to do some more shopping so I left him in town but he's coming around tonight."

"I'm glad. I think you two make a good couple, and I think he's good for you."

"By the way, what did you two talk about when you were leaving my place this morning?"

A silence fell on the line, followed by a shrill laugh which boomed out from the phone.

"What did he tell you?" asked Brett.

"It doesn't matter what he told me, what did you tell him?"

"I just told him about us. That we'd had a great time in Berlin."

"And?"

"Well … that we'd had sex."

"How could you, Brett?"

"But it's true. I told him that it was the first time that I'd had sex with a man and I wanted to have it with someone who meant something to me, and that was you."

"Did you say anything else?" queried Mike.

"Just that you had enjoyed being screwed and so did I."

"Did you say anything about me wanting to be possessed by a man?"

"I might have, why?"

"Alan said that he understood an issue that I had, and that issue was that I liked being screwed by masculine guys and that I loved to be screwed by you. He's right, of course, but he fully understands my situation and is accepting of it."

"So what's wrong with that? Listen Buddy, you've got the best of both worlds just like I have. I've got Belinda when I want a woman, and you when I want a man; and you've got Alan to make love to and when you need to be fucked, you've got me. Don't take it out on the guy, he loves you, and it's time that you had a steady relationship with someone, and I think that someone should be Alan."

Mike listened attentively to Brett and what he said was true, it was just that everything was happening so rapidly. However, he didn't want to dwell on this topic too long, so he changed it.

"Why did you phone, Brett? Have you got some news, because I've got some for you, other than about Alan and me?"

"Yes. I've gone through our records and there's no reference to anyone by the name of Bruno having a record, so I'm not sure where the name came from."

"I'm sure it was Bruno," replied Mike, "but I could be wrong. However, Alan and I went on the big wheel this morning and as we were descending, both of us saw the hunk standing below the wheel. He disappeared before we reached the bottom, but as we got closer both of us saw him smile at us."

"Smile at you?"

"Yep, and that's never happened before."

"Don't flatter yourselves," chuckled Brett.

"Do you think he's mocking us in some way?"

"I don't think so. Perhaps he's just trying to be friendly."

"Are you being serious, Brett? If you are, then what about our hunk being a ghost?"

"Ha, ha, ha!" Brett couldn't control his laughter.

"Think about it," persisted Mike. "Every time we get near him he disappears, and why has nobody else seen him? Why has he not revealed himself to you? You come to the gym. Maybe he is a ghost."

"Well then consider yourself lucky that you're probably the first guy to be fucked by a ghost." There was even more laughter coming from Brett, so much so, that even Mike began to see the funny side and joined in the laughter.

"That's what I like to hear buddy, your laughing, cheery voice. That's the Mike I know. So chill, and don't worry about a thing."

They completed their conversation and Mike went back to his planned afternoon nap. He fell onto the bed again and closed his eyes. Thoughts flashed through his mind. He thought of Alan and the enjoyable time they'd spent today. He thought of Brett and what he and Alan had discussed regarding Mike. He thought of the hunk and the effect his appearances was having on him, but he never thought of work. What a pleasure not to be at work for a change – to be able to do nothing. Sleep was slow in coming but eventually it came. Mike's eyes were heavy and he managed to empty his mind of thoughts and drifted off to a deep sleep.

It was only the constant pounding on his front door that eventually awoke him. He staggered to his feet and in his half asleep daze, he made his way to the door. He opened the door and there stood Steven, his boss.

Fortunately for Mike, he had been sleeping so he wasn't looking wide-awake when he opened the door.

"I just thought I'd pop round to see how you were feeling," called Steven, sounding hale and hearty.

Mike suddenly realized that he was supposed to be off sick, or not feeling well. He thanked God that Steven hadn't called while he and Alan were shopping in town, because that would have taken some explaining.

"Oh, come in Steven. I've been on the bed most of the time, but I'm feeling much better, thanks."

Steven walked past Mike at the doorway and made his way to the lounge, which he could see from the entrance. Mike thought it a bit odd that the boss should come to see how he was feeling. After all, he didn't do that for other trainers or staff. Steven immediately looked around the room.

"Nice place you've got here, Mike. Who did your decorations?"

Mike wasn't too sure whether Steven was being complimentary or sarcastic about his décor.

"I did," was the abrupt reply.

"Nice, nice."

He moved around the room inspecting everything that he laid his eyes on. Mike wondered whether Steven was trying to find out something about him, such as if he lived alone and if not, with whom he lived. This idea infuriated Mike. How dare he question Mike's living arrangements? Mike then thought that he was being childish in his thoughts and it may not be what Steven was trying to find out.

"What exactly is the problem, Mike?"

Mike thought very quickly.

"Stomach! I think I ate something last night that didn't agree with me."

"Ah, not something life-threatening."

Again Mike felt insulted by this man, but he remained calm. This was his boss that he was speaking to and he didn't want to upset the man.

"Well that depends on whether you mean the poisoned food could be life-threatening or whether I had some life-threatening illness like cancer."

Steven gave a snigger and brushed Mike's comment aside.

"How many bedrooms, Mike?"

Oh God, thought Mike, now Steven was venturing into the bedroom area.

"Two," he replied, trying to sound unenthusiastic, hoping that Steven, if he genuinely cared, would see that Mike was not feeling up to this interrogation and would leave.

"Do you often have people stay over?"

What had this to do with his welfare thought Mike, and what did this man actually want?

"Not often, but when I do I have the extra space available for them," was Mike's curt answer.

Mike could see that Steven was itching to be given a Cook's guided tour of the apartment, but he was as determined not to satisfy the man's desires. Mike looked at his watch and saw that it was 6.00 p.m. Alan would soon be arriving and it looked as though Steven had no intentions of leaving just yet. Steven kept up the small talk and Mike actually began to wish he were sick, sick enough to vomit and then that might chase Steven away.

At 6.30 p.m on the dot, the doorbell rang. Mike froze for a moment wondering whether it was Alan or someone else. He ventured to the front door and opened it. Alan stood on the threshold. Mike put on one of his terrified looks and winked to Alan.

"I'm so glad that you were able to come round. I'm feeling much better now, but I still have to be careful what I eat in case my stomach plays up again."

All this was said very loudly, for Steven's benefit as much as Alan's. Alan looked a little puzzled by what Mike was saying, but fortunately, he played along. As he entered the lounge he saw Steven and realized the game Mike was playing. He had brought some food from Marks and Spencer's and carried his overnight bag with him. Alan saw Steven take cognizance of what he was carrying.

"I popped into Marks and Spencer's to get you a little light food for your stomach, Mike."

And then holding the overnight bag up he said, "I also did your washing for you. Shall I put it in your bedroom?"

Mike smiled his best 'sick' smile and thanked Alan.

"I'm glad to see your friends look after you," commented Steven as he watched Alan take the bag into Mike's bedroom. Alan placed his bag on Mike's bed then returned to the lounge.

Mike and Alan didn't say much, trying rather to create a tense atmosphere, which might encourage Steven to leave. It worked. After sitting for about fifteen minutes without very much being said, it became apparent to Steven that his company was not really appreciated, so he left and Alan and Mike were able to spend the evening together.

Chapter 15
GEOFF AND PAVEL

A long weekend was coming up and Alan and Mike were making plans for it. Unfortunately they were not going to be able to go away as on the Saturday night there was to be an important bodybuilding contest to be held in London and Mike was required to work there. Brett was going to Belinda's family for the weekend, so he was excluded from any of their plans.

Some of the staff at the gym had been asked if they were willing to host some of the out-of-town bodybuilders as it would save on hotel accommodation. Mike had spoken to Alan before making a decision. Although they still remained in their separate apartments, they now always consulted one another. Alan had said that he had no objections if Mike wanted to let out his spare room to a couple of the bodybuilders, but he did say that he'd like to stay at Mike's for the weekend. If Mike were agreeable, this would mean that a maximum of two bodybuilders could be accommodated at Mike's.

Mike spoke to Steven at the gym, and it was arranged that two of the entrants would be put up at Mike's apartment. Closer to the time a list of the entrants was sent to Steven who then distributed the names of the people to their various host families. He called Mike into his office and handed him a piece of paper with the names of his two guests.

"Hi Alan," said Mike, phoning from the gym through to Alan's office. "I've got the names of our guests. They're both arriving on Friday evening, but we don't have to supply dinner on the first night. They're going to be here Friday and Saturday and then leave on the Sunday morning. After that, we've got the place to ourselves. How's that grab you?"

"Who are the two guys, do you know them?"

"I've never heard of either," answered Mike, "but their names are Pavel Hanak and Geoff Aston. Apparently Pavel is from the Czech Republic and Geoff is from the USA."

"Sounds like a little United Nations if you ask me," teased Alan. "It could be quite an interesting weekend having two international people to stay. Do you think we should give them international cuisine?"

"Don't joke, they take this sort of stuff seriously. They'll probably have their own diets and foods, but we'll check when they arrive."

"Where are you meeting them, Mike?"

"They're being brought from the airport to the gym and then they will be taken to their various venues from here. You don't have to worry I'll bring them home when I come home from work on Friday. When are you going to come around?"

"I thought I'd go from the office straight round to your place, if that's okay with you?"

"Sure, you can tidy up if you get there before me."

The two men continued to chat about things in general and then they hung up. Mike went into Steven's office.

"Do you know anything about my guests who are coming for the competition?" he asked Steven.

"Not much, except what's on the information sheet that they sent me."

He took the sheet from one of his drawers and looked up the two names.

"Aston, Geoff: twenty-eight, five foot eleven, has won a couple of regional finals. That's all. The other one is Hanak, Pavel. This one's twenty-four, six foot three and it looks like he's also won some local competitions in the Czech Republic. Other then that, I've got no extra information."

Mike made a mental note of the information and then left his boss's office.

On the Friday of the long weekend, the visitors started to arrive at the gym and Mike watched with interest as each person arrived, in an attempt to see if he could find his guests.

When they had all arrived, they were assembled in the main gym area where Steven proceeded to explain to them what was going to happen. The visitors would be taken home by their hosts; then on Saturday morning, they would return to the gym for preliminaries. These would be followed in the afternoon with more judging and then in the evening, they would be taken to Earls Court Exhibition Center for the final judging.

Mike surveyed the group of men, many of whom were tall, so it was difficult for him to identify his guests. As the guests' names were called they would go to Steven who would then introduce them to their host. Eventually, Mike heard the names Hanak and Aston called out. He eagerly watched to see which two men moved towards Steven.

Mike was pleased by what he saw. A tall, good-looking, blonde with a V-shaped back and slim hips moved towards Steven, then he was followed by an equally good-looking, African-American with a shaven head and bulging muscles, the sort that bend iron bars with ease.

Mike moved to the two men. Although he was well built, he seemed almost inadequate and puny next to these men. He introduced himself to them and helped them carry their belongings to the car. Both men spoke easily, although Pavel's English was a little broken and he sometimes used the incorrect word to say something, but as far as Mike was concerned, his looks made up for his linguistic deficiency.

All three men were very animated as they drove to Mike's apartment. When they arrived there, Alan had already arrived and was busy sorting out snacks and drinks for the visitors. With introductions over, and their luggage taken to their room, the four men sat down to relax.

"Mike tells me that you attend his gym, Alan," drawled the American.

"Yes, but I'm not the serious bodybuilder type. I go just to keep in trim," replied Alan.

"And you must see how trim he is," chirped Mike, always willing to praise his friend.

"Oh you must show us sometime," came the slow drawl.

Pavel had sparkling blue eyes, which blended with his strikingly blonde hair. Even as he sat relaxed, one could see the muscles rippling under his T-shirt. He smiled at Alan and asked, "You stay here as well?"

Alan smiled back. "Sometimes. We're friends," he said, pointing to Mike.

Pavel's eyes lit up and his smile broadened. "I see. That is good."

Each guest said that he wanted to freshen up, so Mike showed them where the bathroom was and told them that while they showered, he and Alan would prepare dinner for them, even though it wasn't part of the deal for the first night. Both men were extremely grateful to Mike for his offer.

Geoff was the first to shower and while he was doing that, Mike and Alan busied themselves in the kitchen. Pavel went to the bedroom to unpack.

"Oooh!" exclaimed Alan, almost like an excited schoolgirl, "they're big and gorgeous, aren't they?"

"Control your hormones, you horny thing."

"But they are beautiful. Have you ever seen such bodies, even with their clothes on?"

Mike smiled at Alan's comment, but had to agree with him.

They continued to chat light-heartedly in the kitchen until Geoff walked in with merely a towel wrapped around his waist. Alan nearly dropped the pan he was holding when he saw Geoff's well-defined body.

"I'm sorry to trouble you like this, but I seem to have forgotten my deodorant at home and I wondered if you had some that I could use?"

"Sure, Geoff, I'll give you some of mine," replied Mike, stopping what he was doing and taking Geoff to his bedroom. Alan just stared at the well-defined body that was encased in white toweling, passing by him.

As they passed through the lounge to get to Mike's bedroom, Pavel came out of the second bedroom, just in a pair of briefs and headed towards the bathroom. Mike stopped suddenly and looked. If Michelangelo had carved the statue of 'David', then he must have used Pavel as his model, except Mike could see from Pavel's briefs that he was better endowed than 'David'.

He felt a rush to the head and at the same time a rush to his cock. He quickly took control of himself and resumed his journey to the bedroom. As Geoff followed him into the bedroom, Geoff couldn't help looking around and admiring the décor. Geoff also noted the large double bed. He didn't comment, but his mind worked out that there were only three beds in the apartment, two in the spare room and one in here, but four occupants. Mike offered him a selection of deodorants from which Geoff made a choice.

"Take that one and you and Pavel can use it if you need," said Mike offering the deodorant to Geoff.

Mike then returned to the kitchen while Geoff went to his bedroom to dress.

"You've got to see Pavel," remarked Mike in hushed tones to Alan when he got back in the kitchen. "He's like the inimitable Greek God. What a body."

"Now who's a horny devil?"

When both guests had dressed they returned to the lounge to wait for their dinner. They were casually dressed in shorts, but encasing those bodies, these became short shorts, and white vests, which complemented them. Neither Mike nor Alan could concentrate on either their food or the conversations. All four men were very relaxed and the way they interacted, one would think that they had known each other for years. After dinner, while Alan washed the dishes, the other three remained in the lounge chatting. Eventually Alan joined them and they continued talking about where they came from, the competition and how great it was to be in London. Eventually sleep got the better of the men and Geoff was the first to wander off to bed, quickly followed by the other three.

Mike and Alan made their way to Mike's double bed, stripped off and threw their naked bodies onto the bed and under the duvet and were soon in pleasant dreamland.

Chapter 16
THE PRELIMINARIES

Mike was the first to rise on Saturday morning. He was busy making breakfast in the kitchen when a sleepy-eyed Pavel wandered in to greet him. Pavel had obviously spent the night sleeping in his white briefs and from the view that Mike had, it was like a feast in the morning. Pavel had obviously woken up with an erection and didn't bother to allow it to subside before entering the kitchen. Instead he wandered into the kitchen with a slowly subsiding hard-on. Mike could see from the protrusion in the front of his briefs, that when Pavel was hard, he had a very large cock.

At no time did Pavel show any embarrassment. In fact he stood talking to Mike and rubbing his hand over his crotch and scratching his balls. Little did he know the pain that he was putting Mike through with his physical actions.

Mike's concentration was soon to be shattered again with the arrival of Geoff. He had slept in his shorts and had also woken with a semi-hard-on. So tight were Geoff's shorts that Mike could see the outlined circumcised head of his cock lying down the left leg. Both bodybuilders seemed oblivious of their arousals, but Mike was well aware of his own arousal that was taking place. The three sat and chatted casually in the kitchen, and then as a special treat for Alan, Mike asked Pavel if he wouldn't mind waking Alan, as breakfast was ready. He wanted his friend to see this 'David' in all his glory. Pavel gladly obliged.

Alan was sprawled across the double bed, naked, having kicked the duvet off the bed. Pavel entered the main bedroom quietly and crossed to Alan's sleeping body. With the tenderness of a child, he gently shook Alan's arm to wake him. Alan was sleeping on his back, breathing gently and he too had an erection. His cock was fully erect when Pavel shook him.

"Wake up Alan," whispered the Czech.

He shook him a little more briskly the second time and Alan opened his eyes. He looked straight up into the soft blue eyes of Pavel. Pavel smiled and a row of perfectly formed, white teeth showed. Alan smiled back.

"It's time to get up, but I think you're already up," smiled Pavel.

Alan looked down at his swollen cock, and in embarrassment, covered his crotch with his hands.

"Do not worry," comforted Pavel, "I wake up every morning like that; it is nothing unusual for me."

Alan felt a little comforted by this revelation, but he still kept himself covered. The more he looked at and admired Pavel's body, the less he was able to get rid of his hard-on.

In sheer desperation, he told Pavel to go on ahead and tell Mike that he would soon be there for breakfast.

Alan pulled on a pair of running shorts and soon joined the others for breakfast, but neither he nor Pavel made any mention of his embarrassment.

After breakfast, Mike took Geoff and Pavel to the gym for the first round of the competition. Alan was spending the day at Mike's apartment and was only going to accompany Mike to the finals in the evening.

The gym was a mass of oiled, gleaming bodies, some tall and some short, depending on the groupings. People were pumping up their muscles while others helped oil each other's backs. Once they got to the gym, Pavel and Geoff disappeared to get changed while Mike went to meet Steven and be allocated his job for the competition. Mike's job was to call the contestants at the back of the stage area that had been built. This meant that he got to see all the men first hand. There were various age groups as well. There were very young guys and older men, but all, in Mike's opinion, perfectly built.

The judges were introduced and the preliminary judging began. Mike's job was to call each entrant and see that there was a constant flow of bodies. Each contestant went in front of the judges and did his routine for them, showing off his arms, backs, legs, chests, stomachs, and crotches. Although cocks were not part of the areas to be judged, Mike was making his own judgment as each contestant passed him in his posing brief. For some, Mike wondered how the flimsy material was able to hold such packages in place without them falling out. Each contestant was evaluated individually, and then they were brought out in groups, where it was possible to draw comparisons between them. Mike was impressed with both Pavel's and Geoff's performances and thought that they had both done well.

After a lunch break, the men were back at it posing again. All this was being done to eliminate certain contestants, so that only the best in the various groups remained for the final that evening.

At the end of the afternoon session, the judges announced a list of names of those who had made it through to the final. Mike was overjoyed when both Pavel and Geoff's names were called to go through to the final.

The two bodybuilders showered and got dressed after the session and the three of them headed for home, elated with their success so far.

Back at Mike's apartment, Alan was busying himself in the kitchen when they arrived.

"How did it go guys?"

Mike strutted into the kitchen. "They're both through," he announced proudly.

Alan congratulated both men and resumed his tasks.

"If you don't mind, Mike, I think I'd like a little lie down before we do tonight's event."

"The same here," echoed Pavel.

"Of course. Make yourselves at home. You do whatever you want. We have to be there by 7.00 p.m., so if you fall asleep, I'll wake you," said Mike, patting both men on the shoulder.

The two went off to their bedroom, leaving Mike and Alan alone in the kitchen.

"How's your day been?" asked Mike, putting his arms around Alan's waist and kissing him.

"Fine thanks," was a slightly cool response, "but I need to speak to you."

"Sure, about what?"

Alan pulled from his pocket a small sachet containing some white powder.

"This!" he said, sotto voce, holding the sachet up to Mike.

"What's that?" he asked, looking puzzled.

"I'm sure you know what it is. Cocaine," He hissed the word with contempt as he said it.

"Cocaine!" exclaimed Mike rather loudly. "Cocaine," he whispered, toning his voice down. "Where did you get it from?"

Alan walked to a vase, which stood over the fireplace in Mike's lounge and picked it up.

"Under there," he said, pointing to the now vacant area under the base of the vase.

"But who would have put it there?" enquired Mike, concernedly.

"You tell me, Mike. Are you doing drugs behind my back?"

"No Alan, I'd never do drugs. I hate them," he protested. "You've got to believe me, I would never do drugs."

"I do believe you, Mike, but if it's not yours, then whose is it?"

Mike thought for a time then said almost nonchalantly, "It wouldn't be Pavel or Geoff."

"Why not?" came the question. "I've heard that many bodybuilders do drugs!"

"Yes and so do many wealthy, spoiled kids."

"Are you insinuating something, Mike?"

Having realized what he'd said, Mike apologized profusely to Alan and said that he wasn't suggesting that Alan took drugs but other wealthy, bored kids did.

"I really don't believe those two guys would do it; it would ruin their careers if they were found out," continued Mike.

"Well who put it there? Who else have you had here while I've not been around?"

"Alan, trust me on this one, no one's been here, only you, and I know it's not yours."

A stony silence fell upon the kitchen as the two men stared at each other, waiting for a solution to their problem to arise.

"Well, do we put it back and see what happens?" came Alan's suggestion, breaking the silence.

"You mean to see if either of our guests removes it?"

"Yes, then perhaps we'll get to the bottom of this."

"I don't think so," replied Mike.

"And what if one of them did plant it there and comes back to get it and it's gone, then what?"

"I still don't think it's theirs," persisted Mike.

"Well I'm going to flush it down the toilet," said Alan, striding towards the bathroom.

As he neared the bathroom, Geoff emerged from it in his familiar tight white shorts, having been to the toilet.

"Anything the matter?" he asked, seeing Alan's stern appearance.

"Nothing," snapped Alan, as he side-stepped the bodybuilder and closed the bathroom door behind him. A minute later, the toilet flushed and Alan emerged once more and headed for the main bedroom.

"Lover's tiff?" drawled the American, as he entered the kitchen, where Mike was standing.

"Not at all," replied Mike, without realizing the spontaneity of his reply. He blushed, but Geoff merely smiled a warm, knowing smile.

"It happens in the best of families, you know."

It was as though he had brushed Mike's response aside.

"Relationships are not all plain sailing you know," he continued.

"I'm finding that out," said Mike relaxing to the American.

"I take it that you two are an item. Have you been together long?"

"No, and in fact this is my first relationship with a guy."

Geoff looked stunned.

"Ever?" His voice was raised an octave in disbelief.

"Sure," was the subdued reply, as though Mike had done or said something derogatory.

"But I can't believe a guy as good looking as you hasn't had one before."

"Thanks for the compliment, but no this is my first."

"Well, dog gone! Fancy that."

Mike thought it appropriate to reciprocate.

"What about you, Geoff? Are you in any sort of relationship?"

"Oh yeah. My partner and I have been together for six years. We met at college."

"That's a long time to be together."

"Sure is and we're as happy as a clam."

"It's great to hear when couples have been together for a long time. I hope that Alan and I can make it work for us."

"I'm sure you can. He seems a nice guy. Not exactly what I thought someone like you would go for, but then that's just my opinion."

"Why what sort would you think I would go for?" asked Mike, a little surprised at Geoff's comment, but now showing some serious interest in the American.

"Oh, I don't know. Being a bodybuilder like you, I would have thought that you would go for someone with more bulk, if you catch my drift!"

"Alan's got a very trim body, in fact many have complimented him on his abs, and I find him incredibly sexy."

"I know what you mean about the sexy," whispered Geoff, grinning at Mike. "No, it's just that I could see you with someone like me or Pavel, really well-built."

Mike's cock gave a sudden twitch at the suggestion made by Geoff. Was he making a pass, Mike wondered? Mike could once again feel himself blush. Geoff noticed.

"Oh, but I'm embarrassing you now."

This made Mike blush even more now that Geoff had noticed. It also sent gallons of blood running in the direction of his hardening cock. Mike turned his back on Geoff in the pretext that he wanted to do something at the kitchen sink and slid his hand into his Lycra shorts and adjusted the lie of his cock.

"Problem there, buddy?"

Mike turned to face Geoff, still blushing. Geoff looked down at the swollen crotch that confronted him and a wry smile broke on his face.

"That looks like a hefty package that you're carrying there, buddy. Maybe someone should help you to lighten the load."

His eyes twinkled as he said these words and his own hand slid down over his firm, flat stomach and ran over the protrusion forming in the front of his white shorts. Mike's eyes followed the movement of Geoff's hand and became mesmerized when it reached the crotch area. Geoff leaned back against a work table in the kitchen and thrust his pelvis upwards. Mike gave a gasp as he saw the bulge strain against the soft white material. What if Alan walked in? He had to stop this.

"What if…" began Mike.

"… If Alan walks in," said Geoff, finishing the sentence. "Why not let's ask him?"

Mike panicked. How would he approach Alan after what had happened earlier and say, "How about you, me and Geoff having sex together!"

"It's not right," said a flustered Mike. "What about your relationship?"

"We have an open relationship," retorted Geoff, "but I can see that package growing even bigger and needing some attention."

He gave another thrust of the pelvis and with a wicked grin said, "You want this don't you?"

Mike's mouth was becoming parched. He licked his lips, still staring at Geoff's equally growing member. The temptation was becoming too great. He moved slowly towards where Geoff stood, but this time he was focused on Geoff's eyes. They seemed to burn into Mike. The words 'you want this' kept repeating over and over in his head. Like in a hypnotic trance, Mike reached where Geoff was standing. The two men stood staring into each other's eyes. Geoff stretched out and took Mike's hand and slowly slid it down his chest, guiding it until it reached the waistband of his white shorts, which seemed to glow whiter against the darkness of his skin. Geoff hesitated, and then resumed guiding Mike's hand over the swollen bulge in his shorts. As Mike felt the hard stem and ran his hand over the ridge of Geoff's cock, he closed his eyes and it felt like heaven. He rested his hand there while Geoff removed his, then he gave Geoff's cock the gentlest of squeezes. A sigh, more like a deep breath came from Geoff's lips.

"Do you like that feel?" whispered Geoff.

"Yes," breathed Mike almost silently.

"Do you want it?" whispered Geoff in the closeness of Mike's ear.

"Yes," came the breathless reply.

"Then take it."

Mike sank to his knees in front of Geoff, pulling his shorts down to his ankles at the same time. Geoff's cock bobbed in front of Mike's face. Geoff leaned back against the counter and thrust his hips upwards. His cock rubbed across Mike's face. Mike immediately put out his tongue to lick its length.

Mike worked his mouth up the stem, nipping at it as he did so. When his mouth reached the mushroom head, he lathered it with his tongue and then wrapped the warm cavity of his mouth around it. Slowly his mouth sank down Geoff's length, swirling his tongue around it as he continued his downward journey. Mike opened the back of his throat in order to take Geoff's full length in one go. He felt his chin hit Geoff's balls indicating that he reached the base of his cock. He held that position, letting his tongue now do the work. Geoff groaned audibly and thrust upwards.

Their journey down the yellow brick road to orgasmic fantasy was suddenly shattered by a sneeze from Alan as he made his way towards the kitchen. Mike shot to his feet, pulling Geoff's shorts up as he did so. Geoff desperately tried to hide his erection, but in those tight shorts, it was extremely difficult. Mike busied himself at the sink and both men tried to get their breathing back to a normal pace.

"Hi Geoff," called Alan as he entered the kitchen.

Both Geoff and Mike turned their backs on Alan so that he couldn't see their raging erections.

"What's cooking?" asked Alan, sounding a great deal more cheery than he had a little while earlier.

"I'm just sorting out some food for the guys," stammered Mike.

"Good, do you need a hand?" asked Alan.

Mike and Geoff's eyes met and on hearing Alan's offer, they nearly burst out laughing.

They could quite easily have had an extra hand to help them on their way to ecstasy.

"I think I'd better go and wake up Pavel," said Geoff making to move. His erection had subsided, so he thought it safe to face Alan.

"Oh you don't need to do that, he's sitting in the lounge."

Geoff and Mike again looked at each other. How long had Pavel been sitting there and did he see them in the kitchen? Come to think of it, did Alan see them?

All four men showered, ate and dressed to go to Earl's Court for the final. Mike had suggested that they go out after the competition, but Geoff had suggested they wait and see if they felt like it after the event was over.

Pavel and Geoff had their sweat pants on and each had on a white vest, showing off their physiques. Mike had slipped into his favorite pair of jeans, which fitted snugly around his butt and hips. Alan walked out of the bedroom, surprising everyone, in his leather jeans and a T-shirt, which emphasized his abs. Mike, stared admiringly at his partner. He looked stunning. In fact all three men looked stunning in Mike's eyes. He smiled at them, turned and headed for the front door, but not before he was overheard by them to say, "Let's get going before somebody gets raped here."

Chapter 17
THE COMPETITION

The Earl's Court venue was packed with spectators when they arrived. Mike dropped Pavel and Geoff at the entrance, wished them both good luck and he and Alan went off to find parking. They found some parking a little way from the entrance and then walked back to take their seats. At the final, Mike was not expected to work, so he was able to sit with Alan.

There was an excited buzz coming from the audience. People were chatting animatedly amongst themselves, while ushers ran to and fro, escorting people to their seats. Mike and Alan found their seats quite easily, four rows from the front and made themselves comfortable. This was an ideal spot as they were close enough to see the finer structures of the bodybuilders' muscles and definition. Alan also seemed excited by the whole event as he'd never been to a competition like this before and was very chatty. He leaned sideways towards Mike and whispered in his ear, "I flushed it down the toilet."

"What?"

"The white powder," whispered Alan.

Mike smiled, but it still concerned him as to where the cocaine had come from.

"Thanks, but I still can't think where it came from."

Music blared over the loudspeakers and this competed with the general hubbub of the people. Mike squeezed Alan's leg and whispered, "You look great."

Alan grinned from ear to ear and replied, "But I always look great!"

The two men had a warm feeling between them and they sat back to enjoy the evening's entertainment. The Master of Ceremonies came on stage and welcomed everyone to the event. He then explained the program for the evening and everyone settled back to enjoy themselves.

First up were the juniors. There were some extremely good-looking young men amongst them, with some extremely well-developed physiques. Alan and Mike couldn't help but smile when they saw some of these young studs, admiring the erotic vision in front of them.

"I can see that this is going to be a very difficult evening for both of us," said Alan, with a perfectly straight face and a pompous voice.

"And why is that, may I ask?" replied Mike, equally straight-faced and pompous.

"My dear sir, can you not see what is before you?"

"Absolutely, my dear sir, beautiful young men!"

Alan dropped the pompous voice and in a stage whisper said, "No you fool, my hard-on."

Mike dropped his eyes to Alan's crotch and there he saw the start of Mount Vesuvius beginning to rise.

"Oh God, I hope we make it through this show," was all that Mike could say, and burst out laughing.

A few people turned their heads to see what was so funny; forcing Mike to straighten his face and stop laughing.

Following on after the juniors, the seniors, according to weight, began to parade. Both men sat forward in their seats in an effort to get a better view. Pavel was in a lighter weight group than Geoff, so he would come on stage sooner.

They didn't have to wait long for Pavel to appear on stage. He looked magnificent in his pale blue, satin posing briefs. His body was oiled and he gleamed in the bright stage lights. Yes, he truly was a Greek God! He posed showing off the definition that he had acquired in training, flexing almost every muscle that existed in his body. Somehow, Mike thought that he looked bigger now than he had earlier in the afternoon. When Pavel finished his routine, the entire Earl's Court rose to their feet and cheered and applauded. People whistled and shouted; some even stamped their feet on the floor to create extra noise.

When they had completed their individual routines, the contestants were brought out in groups, so that comparisons could be made by the judges. Mike and Alan felt proud of their guest.

"Doesn't he look great against those others," remarked Alan.

"I think he's the best of the group," said Mike applauding wildly.

Alan sidled up to Mike and whispered in his ear, "If you had to choose one, who would it be?"

"Do you mean, who'd be my winner?"

"No, who'd you like to bed?"

Mike did a double take at Alan, then smiled, looked back at the contestants and said, "Number 6."

Alan was taken aback by this response and had to look quickly at the contestants numbers attached to their skimpy posing briefs. His face lit up when he saw that number 6 was Pavel.

Turning to Mike, he winked and said, "So would I."

There was a short break while the next group of contestants prepared for their solo routines.

Backstage, Geoff congratulated Pavel on his wonderful performance and suggested that in his opinion, Pavel was the best of that weight group. Pavel took the compliment in his own modest way, brushing it aside and saying that there were other guys better than him.

Soon it was Geoff's turn. Although he was one of the shortest in his group, physically he looked the best developed. He too went through the motions of his routine, flexing, turning and posing, exposing his taut well-oiled and glistening muscles to perfection. Again the cheer from the crowd for the bodybuilders was deafening. The same procedure followed, that of groups coming onto the stage together.

Mike turned to Alan and asked, "Does the same question apply to this group as before?"

Alan wasn't sure as to what Mike was referring.

"You asked earlier which one of them I'd like to bed. Does the same question apply here?"

"Oh, for sure," came the immediate reply.

Mike again looked at the line–up and said, "Number 4."

Once again, Alan had to search those posing briefs for the contestant's number. Once again, his face lit up. Number 4 was Geoff.

"I'm glad we've got so much in common," sniggered Alan.

Interval was drawing near and just before interval, the winners of the different weight groups would be announced and those winners would go through to a final group to choose the overall winner.

The junior section was won by a dark, young man from Brazil. There were mixed reactions from the crowd because some approved while others thought a German guy should have won, but they were not short in showing their appreciation for the Brazilian man, through their applause.

When the result of Pavel's section was announced, the crowd went wild. Mike and Alan leapt from their seats when Pavel was named as the winner. His blonde hair and his oiled body glowed in the light as he flexed his arms and legs once more for the crowd. At one point Mike thought that Pavel's crotch looked bigger than usual, from the angle at which he was standing. Mike wondered how that skimpy posing pouch was able to contain such a wealth of manhood. Pavel graciously received his trophy and left the stage, smiling his beautiful smile.

Geoff's section was not as cut and dried as people thought it might be. After much deliberation, the judges announced the results. In third place was number 2, from England; second was number 5, from Russia and the winner was number 4 from the USA. Geoff leapt into the air with excitement at the announcement and he too graciously accepted his trophy.

After interval, the section winners paraded once again on stage for the audience and the judges. The giant who won the heavyweight section made the others look minuscule in comparison, but when he looked, Mike thought that perhaps Geoff stood a good chance, as he appeared more defined than the giant. They once again flexed, posed and paraded for the judges, with the crowd cheering their own favorites on all the time.

Finally a decision had been made.

The announcer cleared his throat and spoke clearly into the microphone: "In third place overall, number 6, Pavel Hanak; in second, from the USA, Geoff Aston, and in first place, from France, Jacques Du Pont."

The giant from the heavyweight division had won, but their two friends had made them proud. The audience once again went wild, cheering and whistling. They agreed with the judges' decisions, so as far as everyone was concerned, it had been a fair competition.

Mike and Alan rushed backstage to congratulate their two friends. They heaped praise on both Geoff and Pavel as they hugged each other, ignoring the fact that both bodybuilders were still covered in oil.

When the excitement had begun to subside, Mike suggested the two men get changed and then they could go out and celebrate. Mike and Alan followed Geoff and Pavel into the change rooms to wait for them. The smell of baby oil and testosterone took Alan's breath away, not to mention the sight of so many naked and half-naked young men, preening in front of each other.

Pavel slipped his posing pouch down to his ankles and stepped out of them. He turned to enter the shower and Mike saw the beautiful, nine-inch, pendulous cock swaying from side to side as he walked. Mike could see the wrinkles of foreskin, which covered the head, pulled together forming a spout. Mike envisaged his mouth around that cock, slowly pushing the folds of foreskin back to reveal a waiting head.

"Wait for me Pavel," shouted Geoff as he jogged towards his buddy, his cock bouncing as he did so. Mike turned to look at Alan, whose mouth was open in wonder. Mike gently cupped his hand under Alan's jaw and pushed his mouth closed.

"Didn't your mother ever tell you it's bad manners to stare, especially with your mouth wide open; you never know what might go in it."

"I know very well what could go in it," answered Alan, punching his buddy on the arm.

After showering and dressing, the four set off to the nearest pub to celebrate. Many drinks later, they stumbled back into Mike's apartment.

Chapter 18
A TASTE OF EACH OTHER

Back at the apartment the trophies were given pride of place on the mantelpiece above the fireplace, once the illustrious vase had been removed.

Mike went into the kitchen to make everyone some coffee while the others collapsed in the lounge. Everyone was light-hearted and slightly inebriated from their celebrations. After some moments, Geoff shouted through to Mike in the kitchen, "Do you need a hand?"

Mike immediately responded with, "I need more than a hand," to which the group burst out laughing. Geoff got up and went into the kitchen, leaving Pavel and Alan chatting together.

Mike was at the sink with his back to Geoff, when he felt the sturdy hands of the bodybuilder wrap around his waist, spin him around and felt the hot mouth encompass his own. He felt Geoff's tongue force entry into his mouth and then he relaxed. His own tongue fought with Geoff's as they ground their hips against each other's. Although Geoff was shorter than him, he could feel the hardness of his cock jabbing into the base of his stomach. Geoff came up for air, "I've got to have you," he gasped and went back to attacking Mike's lips.

This time it was Geoff who made the move and unzipped Mike's jeans. He tore at the Calvin Klein's and pulled Mike's cock out of its hiding place. His foreskin hadn't rolled back yet, as it usually did on these occasions, but it didn't stop Geoff from putting his mouth over its head and nibbling at Mike's foreskin. He inserted his tongue into its folds and then pushed Mike's foreskin back to reveal his pink cock head. Saliva dribbled from Geoff's mouth as he lathered up Mike's cock. Mike leaned back against the draining board of the sink, closed his eyes and went into fantasy world.

Alan and Pavel, who had stopped talking for a while, got up to go to the kitchen to see what was happening to their coffee. The two men got to the entrance to the kitchen and saw Geoff on his knees before Mike, taking Mike's cock deep into his throat, while Mike's head was thrown back and his eyes were closed as in dreamland.

Alan and Pavel smiled to each other.

"So this is how you make coffee?" said Alan. "Maybe, Pavel and I should show you how to do it!"

Geoff and Mike then looked at their ‘visitors’, standing in the kitchen doorway, but soon turned away and resumed their action.

Pavel’s eye glowed with joy when Alan ran a hand over his crotch. He pulled down his sweat pants to reveal his nine-inch monster. Alan immediately dropped to his knees and began to worship Pavel’s appendage. He pushed the tip of his tongue into the folds of foreskin, and with his hand, took Pavel’s stem and slid his hand down to its base, pulling the foreskin back at the same time. Pavel’s foreskin rolled back to reveal the pink bulbous head. Alan licked around the head, flicking his tongue over its top, and then sliding his tongue under its length until his mouth reached Pavel’s balls. Each testicle was gently handled with his tongue, plopping into his mouth, one at a time and gently licking around them, then plopping them out again.

At the sink, Geoff had pulled Mike’s jeans down to his ankles and his mouth was working on the inside of Mike’s groin, lathering each ball with his saliva. The air was thick with sex and each man, in his own way, was groaning with satisfaction. Mike opened his eyes again and watched Alan performing on Pavel. He wanted to be part of that as well. He wanted to enjoy his loved one as much as he was enjoying the other two men. He pulled his wet cock from Geoff’s mouth and said, “Why don’t we go to the lounge or the bedroom?”

Geoff and Alan rose from their kneeling position and all four went into the lounge. As they entered the lounge area, clothes began to disappear; shirts were ripped off and jeans and sweat pants got flung onto the floor; soon all four were naked and romping on the floor. There was no real pairing up at this stage; Pavel moved to Mike, while Geoff swallowed Alan’s throbbing cock; then Mike and Alan were together while Pavel kissed and fondled Geoff. However in each one’s mind some sort of planning must have been taking place, because after some time of rolling around on the carpet, Geoff stood up, went into his bedroom and returned carrying a handful of condoms and two tubes of lube.

“Mike, I want you to screw Alan. Show us how much you love him,” said Geoff standing over the others on the floor. He threw a condom to Mike. Mike smiled up at him, not knowing what the overall plan was. Mike tore the foil and rolled the condom down his erect cock.

“Pavel, lube up the kid,” was Geoff’s next command.

Alan hadn’t been called a kid for many years, but amongst this group, he was the youngest and had the slightest physique so he wasn’t about to argue with Geoff. Pavel squeezed some of the lube onto his fingers and gently probed Alan’s ass, finding his pink entry and inserting not one but two fingers. Alan gasped when the fingers entered him but it brought with it a sense of lust. Pavel wiggled his fingers around inside Alan, driving the young man crazy with desire to have something thicker in that cavity. Geoff swept everything from the marble coffee table and told Alan to lie down on it. Alan did as he was told and raised his legs to reveal his shaved rosebud.

“Now show me how you make love,” he said, pushing Mike to between Alan’s legs.

Mike held the stem of his cock and aimed for his target. Alan’s eyes never left Mike’s face. He felt the round head touch his opening and prepared for the onslaught. Mike was gentle and slow with his entry, allowing Alan to get used to his length and girth. When he felt his lover was ready, Mike started a slow rhythmic thrust, which made Alan slide a little on the table.

Pavel, who had been watching all the time, placed his hand with the excess of lube on Geoff’s bouncing cock and started a slow movement up and down its length, in time to Mike’s thrusts. This continued for a while with the two bodybuilders watching every thrust and pull.

Geoff then snapped a command. “Mike pull out and come here. Pavel take his place.”

Mike did as he was commanded, and Pavel, having placed a condom on his cock, slid into the warmth of Alan. Alan grunted as Pavel made his first thrust, as his cock was longer than Mike's, but Mike had loosened Alan up, ready for Pavel's weapon.

Mike crossed to Geoff.

"Suck my big dick," commanded Geoff, "but I want you to watch your lover being fucked at the same time."

Every time that Geoff issued a command, Mike felt his cock throb. Every time he watched what was happening around him, his cock throbbed.

Mike did as he was commanded, tasting the lube that Pavel had used on Geoff's cock, and watched as Pavel thrust deeply into Alan. He could see Alan perspiring, but lying there with a satisfied glow on his young face. Pavel leaned forward while thrusting, and kissed Alan gently on the lips, their tongues becoming entwined.

While Mike worked on Geoff's cock, Geoff grabbed his hair and pulled his face away from his cock.

"You like to be fucked don't you?" sneered Geoff.

"Yes," murmured Mike.

"I didn't hear you."

"Yes," said Mike with a raised voice.

Geoff pulled his cock from Mike's mouth and strode over to the coffee table. He grabbed Pavel by the shoulder as though to indicate that he pull out of Alan.

Geoff moved Alan from the table and told Pavel to lie down on it. Pavel did as he was instructed. "Mike, sit on that fucking cock. Ride that bargepole. That's what you want isn't it?"

Mike's voice almost left him, not out of fear, but out of sheer excitement. He was going to get to ride this Greek God.

Slowly Mike lowered his torso onto Pavel's cock so that he looked into the beautiful face. He felt his sphincter clamp tight, but he soon lost the battle and Pavel's cock broke through. Mike let out a gasp; both of pain and pleasure, then slowly sank down its length until his butt was resting on Pavel's balls.

"Now ride him boy?" barked Geoff.

Throughout this process Geoff continued to play with his dick, stroking it and fumbling with his balls.

"Alan, stand astride Pavel and face Mike. Now Mike, take your man and suck him dry."

Mike opened his mouth to allow Alan's cock to slide in. His ecstasy was rising. A Greek God was fucking him while he was giving pleasure to the man he loved, and Pavel was fingering Alan, all at the same time.

Geoff watched this ménage a rios with interest. His stroking of his dick was becoming more intense; he needed to be satisfied; he needed to be part of this passion. He placed a condom on his dick and moved behind Mike's back. The breathing from the three men on the coffee table was growing in volume, just as the groans and body slaps were. Geoff could sense that they were all getting near the completion of their passion.

Geoff barked an order for Mike to rise to the tip of Pavel's cock, but not to allow it to slip out and to stay in that position until he told him otherwise.

Mike rose up the stiffened length and held his position on the tip. His leg muscles ached from the up and down movement. He felt Geoff's hands push on his back, forcing him to lean forward towards Pavel's chest. Alan adjusted his position when this took place, but never allowed his lover to let go. Mike felt the top of Geoff's dick rub up against his ass- crack. What was the man thinking, wondered Mike? He felt Geoff take hold of his own dick and gently guide it so that it rubbed up against Pavel's. He pushed forward into Mike's ass, but Mike's muscles rebelled. Pavel could also feel the extra cock fighting for entry, but he never withdrew. Finally, Mike's muscles gave in and he cried out in pain as Geoff's dick broke through the sphincter to join Pavel's in the warm cavity. Nobody moved as Mike's cry continued. Geoff, with his free hand rubbed more lube over Mike's opening and the two hard rods impaling him.

"Now this is going to be something special," gasped Geoff, slowly pushing into Mike with Pavel's cock sliding alongside his own.

Alan watched as tears welled up in Mike's eyes. He wanted this to stop because of the pain Mike was enduring, but he was afraid Geoff might do something drastic. As Mike sank back down Pavel's cock, so Geoff pushed deeper. He had never experienced something like this before. Mike's cries soon stopped and he reverted to heavy breathing and pleasurable groans. The pain had been supplanted by joy and pleasure. Both Pavel and Geoff had the looks of well-satisfied men as their cocks slid side by side into Mike's cavity. With the constant friction of his cock by Geoff's, Pavel let them know that he was about to shoot.

"Aaargh!!" gasped Pavel as he thrust deeply into Mike's asshole, every muscle in his body straining as he fired salvo after salvo.

Both Geoff and Mike could feel Pavel's cock throb and jerk with every ejaculation. With sweat pouring from his chest, Geoff thrust into Mike like some wild animal, snorting and grunting uncontrollably as he reached his climax. His muscular body tensed, he gave a cry and fell across Mike's back, thrusting and pushing with each seed that parted from his body.

With two throbbing cocks inside of him, Mike couldn't contain the ecstatic feelings that he was receiving. Mike worked faster on Alan's cock, still warmly encased in his mouth, and with three of Pavel's fingers firmly embedded in Alan's ass; he tried to bring his lover off at the same time that he would come. He frantically rode both subsiding cocks, feeling no pain any more only the desire for absolute pleasure. He could feel his climax racing through his body. He cried out and gasped heavily as he shot his first load onto Pavel's chest. Throughout his eruption, he kept working on Alan. He felt Alan's cock thicken and stiffen and then the sweet salty taste entered his mouth. Alan fired into Mike, holding onto his shoulders as he shot his load while Pavel's fingers remained clamped in the tightness of Alan's rosebud.

Eventually the room became still. Nobody moved. Instead, each luxuriated in the other's warmth. Geoff's soft lips caressed Mike's back, while Mike collapsed across Pavel's stomach, expended. He could feel his warm sticky cum on Pavel's chest which rubbed onto his chest uniting the two of them.

Still holding onto Mike's waist, Geoff slowly withdrew, and when he had, he still held on to Mike, never losing contact. Mike gently raised himself from Pavel until all four were sprawled, limbs linked, on the carpet where they spent the rest of the night in each other's protection.

Chapter 19
THE MORNING AFTER THE NIGHT BEFORE

The following morning found the four still lying on the lounge floor, entwined with each other. Slowly their aching bodies began to awaken. Mike was the first to stretch his body and rise from the floor. He stood up and looked down at the sleeping beauties: Pavel and Geoff with their arms around each other and Alan with his head burrowed into Pavel's chest. Mike bent down and kissed Alan's sleeping face. The first thought that crossed his mind was GUILT! How would Alan feel about what happened the night before? Sure they'd all had a bit too much to drink and were celebrating, but was that reason enough to have done what they did?

In his heart he knew that he and Alan could make a go of their relationship. He knew that their feelings were mutual and that they loved each other. However, watching Pavel make love to Alan was a little disturbing for him. He didn't know how to deal with someone else fucking his lover in front of him, but perhaps this was all a test for him; a test of his love for Alan. Maybe Alan felt the same way about him, but in his mind he knew that whatever had happened the previous night, the only person he had fucked was Alan, and that was something he'd promised his lover, that he wouldn't fuck other guys.

Alan opened his eyes and saw Mike sitting on the couch.

"Hi, babes how are you?" smiled Alan getting up and sitting next to Mike.

"I'm fine, thanks. What about you?"

Alan smiled and nodded his head as if to say that he was okay.

"Thanks for last night. I hope you enjoyed yourself."

Alan kissed him and added, "I sure did, but I felt sorry for you at one stage."

Mike grinned. "Oh you don't have to feel sorry for me. It was painful at first, but then I began to enjoy it. You know I like to be taken by big muscular guys; it's a real turn-on."

"But to have two at once!"

"That I've never had before, but that's what I call really fucked, what about you?

"What do you mean what about me?" enquired Alan. "Do you mean Pavel and me? He's very sexy don't you think, and I'll let you into a little secret, just as you like big muscular guys, I like a big muscular cock, that's why I love you." Mike chuckled at his friend's comment.

"I did feel hurt when Pavel started making love to you, but I could see that you were enjoying it and that made me happy."

"You forget Geoff was clever in getting you to make love to me first, in that way he thought you wouldn't become jealous."

Mike thought about what Alan had just said and realized that perhaps Geoff was testing his love for Alan on the one hand and giving him the pleasure he so enjoyed, of being possessed, on the other.

Pavel and Geoff's bodies stirred and they opened their eyes, finding themselves arm in arm, snuggled up to each other.

"Good morning. Ready for another session?" joked Mike, "Or can't you big guys take the pace."

Geoff guffawed and said, "Any time buddy! I'm ready to start any time," grabbing his dick and giving it a squeeze as if to bring it back to life.

"Put it away Geoff. Any more and it'll fall off," said Pavel smacking at Geoff's dick.

Breakfast was served and everyone got dressed. Pavel and Geoff said that they had decided to remain in the UK for a while longer to tour before returning to their respective homes, so it was decided that Mike and Alan would take them to the station and they would go their own way. They went off to the bedroom to pack their bags while Alan and Mike washed up the dishes.

"I think I'm going to miss them," remarked Alan.

"I know I will, but maybe we'll see them again," replied Mike.

Alan went into the lounge to clean up and spotted Geoff going through their drawers in the main bedroom. He stealthily crept towards the room and peered through the open door. He saw Geoff scratch through one of the bedside tables. He entered the room.

"Can I help you with something, Geoff?"

"No it's okay, thanks Al," he said, closing the drawer. "I was just looking to see if you guys had some spare condoms that we could take on our tour."

Alan wasn't sure whether this was for real or not, but he chose to play along.

"We've got plenty. I'll get you some; after all you've got to play safe these days."

Alan crossed to the wardrobe, opened it and felt around. He pulled a handful of condoms from the cupboard and handed them to Geoff.

"That should keep you going for a day or two."

Geoff thanked him and they both left the bedroom. Alan returned to the kitchen and told Mike what had happened.

"Maybe he was looking for his cocaine," suggested Alan, as they returned from the railway station having dropped the two men and exchanged telephone numbers and addresses with them.

"I still don't think it was them, but yes, I can't give you an answer as to why Geoff really was going through our things. Perhaps the condom story is genuine."

They put their thoughts to rest and settled in for a quiet relaxing Sunday together. Alan had bought a couple of the Sunday papers and they spread them out on the floor in the lounge and started to read. While Mike was reading an article about the competition, which included photos of Pavel and Geoff, it suddenly dawned on him.

"Alan, I think I know who might have left that cocaine under the vase."

"Who?" came a disinterested voice.

"Steven!"

Alan looked up from his newspaper.

"Why Steven?"

"Remember he came round the day I was supposed to be sick and I told you that I thought his coming to see me very odd?"

"I do, but why?"

"That I can't tell you, but he's the only other person who's been in this apartment."

"Do you think that he's trying to set you up for some reason?"

"If he is, I can't think of a reason. I've done nothing to harm or jeopardize his position."

"If it was him, do you think Geoff's story about the condoms is genuine?"

"I honestly don't think either of those two guys put it there and I don't think Geoff was looking for it when you found him in the bedroom."

Alan's concerned expression changed to one of suspicion. "What about the hunk?" he said.

"What about him?" questioned Mike.

"Look, he was here, in your bedroom. Remember the night of your 'dream'; well he could have placed it under the vase!"

Mike had never thought of that, in fact he'd forgotten about that. He didn't respond and both men left the topic there and went back to their newspapers.

At five that afternoon, the phone rang and a cheery voice on the other end said, "Have you two behaved yourselves this weekend?" It was Brett.

"Would we ever," said Mike. "You know what happens when two horny people get together, don't you?"

"Four!" butted in Alan.

"No, I wouldn't know."

"You're right, you're never horny are you; but did you have a good weekend?"

"It was great and Belinda's folks gave us a good time."

"Into geriatrics, now are we?"

The banter continued for some time, each friend trying to outdo the other. Mike told Brett about the competition and how charming the two guests were, but never let on about the foursome they'd had.

Alan got Mike's attention while he was talking and whispered to him: "Don't say anything about the vase."

"What's Alan say?" asked Brett.

"Nothing important, he's just mumbling to himself as usual."

Mike wondered if he should mention the cocaine to Brett, after all he was a cop, but then it struck him that he might accuse them of being in possession. Silence was the better option, but the cocaine episode never left their minds.

Chapter 20
COCAINE

Brett stood at the window of his fifth storey office, looking down on the myriad of people moving hurriedly on the street below. His mind was blank. He thought of no one, nothing; it was truly a dead stare that emanated from his eyes. His secretary entered the room and said something to him, but he was oblivious to her presence or what she had said. The traffic outside added to the hustle and bustle of a Wednesday morning, but in Brett's head he heard no sounds. No thought; no sound, just dead. In the distance he began to hear a ringing, which seemed to get louder and louder and his thoughts slowly returned to him. He was slowly returning to the reality of his office and the world around him. He snatched up the ringing telephone.

"Yes!" was the abrupt response.

His secretary's voice at the other end of the line spoke and then the conversation was over and he returned the phone to its cradle. He looked down on his desk and saw a piece of paper which his secretary had deposited there. He picked it up. On the scrappy piece of paper, held loosely in his hand, he read the words:

COCAINE – 115 Broughton Court – Haverstock Road.

The letters had been individually cut from a newspaper and pasted higgledy-piggledy onto the scrappy piece of paper. It looked unprofessional, but it reminded him of the type one would see in the movies. Brett's eyes scanned the note for any clues. This sort of thing could be sent by anyone, because it just arrived at Brett's office, sans envelope or postal marking.

The address rang bells in his head. He knew Broughton Court very well; he had visited there many times and he knew 115 even better; that was the home of Mike, his best friend. He wondered if this was some sort of prank. Mike wouldn't do cocaine; he prided his body too much and they'd been friends long enough for Brett to know Mike's pleasure habits. However, he couldn't ignore it because the note had already gone through certain police channels, so people were aware of its existence.

His mind wandered back to the pressing crowds on the street below. Mike would probably be at the gym by now. Should he phone him there or personally go round and speak to him. Speaking to him would be the obvious choice for his friend, because he would be able to gauge Mike's reaction to the information. Brett spoke to his secretary and told her that he was going out but didn't say where, placed the scrappy note in his pocket and head off in the direction of the gym.

Mike was busy working with one of his clients doing squats when Brett appeared before him.

"What are you doing here so early?" was the surprised reaction of Mike's.

"Hi Mike, I wanted to speak to you, so I came round now rather than wait until later."

"To want to speak to me this early means that something's wrong. Has something happened to Alan?" questioned Mike, panic suddenly appearing on his face.

"No, Mike. He's fine, so far as I know. Nothing's happened to him, but I need to speak to you in private."

This was sounding very serious to Mike. What had he done to warrant Brett's serious visit so early in the day?

"Come through to my office," said Mike, leaving his client to continue on some other exercises that didn't need Mike's attention.

The two men headed to Mike's office, passing Steven's on the way. The boss merely raised his eyes, noted the two men and then went back to what he was doing.

"Sit Brett; now tell me what's happened." Mike was troubled by this visit and it showed on his face.

The two men sat down opposite each other across Mike's desk.

"Mike, I received this early this morning." He took the scrappy note from his pocket and pushed it across the table for Mike to read. Mike picked it up, read its contents and looked up into Brett's waiting face.

"Where did this come from?" asked Mike.

"I have no idea. I've no idea if it's for real or some sick prank being played on you, but is it true? I need to hear from you before we move in and search your place."

Mike could feel the blood rush to his head; he felt dizzy with shock. Who would do this to him and why?

"Come on buddy, you know you can talk to me," appealed Brett. "Rather me than one of my bullying colleagues."

Mike knew in his mind that he would rather have Brett question him, but he was still transfixed by the note.

"Do you do cocaine, and if so is there some in your apartment, buddy?"

Mike looked Brett squarely in the eyes.

"No, to both counts," replied Mike with confidence and authority in his voice.

Brett knew from Mike's tone that he was being genuine in his answer, but others might not. If he were to arrest him and Mike were tried, others might not believe his sincere "no" answer.

"I believe you Mike, but why would someone send a note like this. They say 'where there's smoke, there's fire' you know?"

"I hear what you say, but don't condemn yet. You've known me long enough to know that I wouldn't take drugs. I'm totally against them, but I can't help you with regard the note. You've got to believe me."

Brett watched his friend's face for any signs, which might suggest that Mike wasn't being truthful, but there were none.

Brett changed his tactic and asked Mike whether he was aware that Alan might be doing drugs. Mike scoffed at the idea.

"He does come from a well-to-do background and you know what they're like?"

Mike became angry at this suggestion.

"No, Brett, I don't know what they're like as you put it, but I do know what Alan's like and he wouldn't touch the stuff if you offered it to him on a silver platter."

"That might be a convenient place to sniff it from, that platter," Brett replied.

"You know, you're making me sick," retorted Mike, now raising his voice in anger.

People who had been walking past Mike's office at the time stopped and looked in through the glass panel.

"I'm sorry, Mike, I'm only doing my job and I want to get to the bottom of this as much as you do. Now is there anything you can tell me as to why someone should create this note?"

Mike eventually relented and began to tell Brett about Alan finding the sachet of cocaine under the vase in the lounge.

"When last did you move that vase, Mike?"

He thought for a while and then said, "Probably three weeks ago, when I was dusting."

"Right now think of the people who you've had in your apartment since then."

"Alan and I were discussing this after we'd found the stuff and the only people we can think of are Pavel and Geoff, the two guys staying with us for the competition, Steven and …" Mike paused.

"Yes?"

"The hunk, if it wasn't a dream!"

"Are you sure about that? Listen if you have perhaps, and I say perhaps, brought somebody else round to your place for whatever reason, tell me. I'm not going to mention anything to Alan."

Mike gave Brett a cold stare.

"If you mean have I been fucking around, the answer's no! I haven't brought anyone else home."

"Okay, so we've got Pavel, Geoff, Steven and the hunk! Now in your honest opinion, do you suspect any of them?"

Mike thought long and hard.

"Alan did see Geoff scratching through a bedside table in our room the day that the two guys were leaving."

"Did you ask Geoff why he was doing that?"

"Alan did, and he said that he was looking for some condoms as he didn't have any left."

"Sounds like it was a busy weekend!"

Mike chose to ignore the innuendo.

"And was he?"

"I don't know," replied Mike, "but I believe Geoff."

"And why would you do that? A stranger in your home; you only met him recently and wouldn't know much about him, so why would you believe him?"

"I can't explain, Brett, but I did. Maybe I'm wrong, but I'm sure that I'm not."

Brett tried another tack.

"What about Steven, then? Why would he plant it?"

"I don't know. Alan and I discussed his possibility, but we can't find a reason for him to do it, and as for the hunk – well I've got his HOM briefs, but I can't see the connection."

Brett listened intently to all Mike's answers and that satisfied him that his friend was telling the truth.

"Look Mike, I'm sorry I had to do this but I needed to put my mind at rest that you weren't doing drugs and neither was Alan. I care for the two of you and you know I want to help, so if you remember anything else, please don't hesitate, any time of the day or night, to call me."

Mike thanked Brett for his concern and the two men shook hands and both returned to their work.

Chapter 21
A NEW MEANING TO GOING TO MOVIES

Mike spent the balance of that Wednesday trying to focus on his job, but found it increasingly difficult to take his mind off the note and the cocaine. At lunchtime, he phoned Alan and told him what had happened, about the visit from Brett and the scrappy note that the police had received. This also worried Alan.

"Do you think we need to get a lawyer?" he asked Mike.

Mike said that he didn't think it was necessary and that he trusted Brett and he was sure that nothing too serious would come of the incident.

"But what if it falls out of Brett's hands and is given to some other detective to investigate, what then?"

"I don't think that's likely to happen," reassured Mike. "I'm sure that Brett will keep the whole thing quiet."

The two men agreed to meet after work, have a drink together and then go to a movie in the evening to try and take things off their minds.

They met at a pub near Leicester Square, had a meal and then went off to the Odeon Cinema to see their movie. They bought their tickets and went in and found their seats. They chatted about the events of the day and settled down for a pleasurable evening.

The cinema was fairly crowded, but in the dim light of the cinema, they could see some empty seats. Alan sat in the seat next to the aisle, with Mike sitting on his left. The lights dimmed a little further and the trailers of forthcoming attractions were shown and still the audience was arriving.

"Excuse me," said a gentleman, wanting to pass Alan and Mike in order to get to his seat in the same row. "Thank you," he said as he passed them both and took his seat next to Mike.

Mike looked at him in the gloomy light. He was about fifty to fifty-five, thickset, bald and with a small moustache, not something that either Mike or Alan would probably look at twice. The man made himself comfortable and he too relaxed to enjoy the film.

Eventually, with the trailers now out of the way, the cinema darkened fully and the main feature film began. It was a thriller. Why they had chosen to watch a thriller, neither of them actually knew because they were not ardent fans of thrillers, but here they were in the darkness of the cinema, ready to be frightened.

They became rapt in the film, surprisingly enjoying it as the story unfolded.

Mike was sitting relaxed in his seat, with his legs apart, when he felt the man on his left touch his leg with his own leg. Mike shifted slightly and continued to watch the film. A little later the two legs again touched. Mike gave the man a sideways glance and then resumed watching the film. About four or five minutes later, the man again touched Mike's leg, but this time didn't move his leg. His eyes stayed fixed on the screen as he felt the man start to rub their legs together. Mike felt this tactile movement stimulating and began to feel movement in the groin area.

As the film progressed, so did the man's advances. Mike was resting his left arm on the armrest when he felt the man's right hand touch his arm. He wasn't sure whether he should move his arm and say something to the man, or leave his arm where it was. He chose to leave his arm on the armrest. He felt the man slide his arm under Mike's and felt a hand touch his hardened crotch. Mike quickly glanced in Alan's direction to see if he was seeing what was going on next to him, but Alan was totally engrossed in the film. Mike, on the other hand, found his concentration in the film waning.

The man's fingers gingerly took hold of the zip on Mike's jeans and slowly and quietly slid it down. The man paused, and then when he thought it safe, inserted his right hand inside Mike's jeans.

Mike could feel the soft hands slide over his hard-on. The hand squeezed his cock gently and rubbed up and down it again. Mike kept watching Alan out of the corner of his eyes, but Alan never reacted to him. Mike adjusted his position so that he had turned his body a little more towards the man, making his hand movements easier for him. The man was now able to grasp the full girth of Mike's cock. Mike felt the hand slide into his briefs and encircle his flesh. The hand was warm as it started a slow and methodical upward and downward movement. Still, Alan remained oblivious to the action, taking place next to him.

Mike could feel that he wanted to come, here in the darkness of the cinema at the hands of a strange man. It seemed to add to the mystery of his already mysterious day.

The hand tightened its grip on his cock, and the movement began to increase. Mike could feel that he was nearing a climax, but where was he to shoot his warm cum? The man continued to bring Mike closer and closer to total pleasure. Suddenly Mike gasped and fired his first shots over the man's hands and into his briefs. Mike coughed to try and cover the sound of his gasp. He felt his briefs becoming more and more wet and sticky as volley after volley of warm cum shot forth. When he was depleted, the man slowly withdrew his cum-covered hand, gently zipped up Mike's jeans, pulled out a handkerchief to wipe his hand and returned his attention to the film. Mike also returned his attention to the film unaware of what was actually going on in the film, because his concentration had been focused elsewhere.

The film ended and with the house lights coming up, Alan and Mike left their seats to head for the exits. Mike turned as he left and gave the man a parting smile, almost as thanks.

"Did you enjoy that?" asked Alan, as they reached the foyer.

"Mmmm! Yes," replied Mike thinking more of the man's action on him than the film.

In the brightness of the foyer, Alan looked at Mike and said, "It looks like it."

Mike frowned at Alan, as he didn't understand what Alan was getting at, and then Alan pointed to Mike's crotch. Mike looked down and saw the dried stains of some of his love juice on the front of his jeans.

"I think you'd better go to the toilet and clean up before we go home," laughed Alan, as Mike sheepishly tried to hide his embarrassment and head for the toilets.

Returning to Alan, who had waited behind in the foyer, Mike's face was a picture of embarrassment as the front of his jeans were wet where he had removed the stains, and now it looked as though he'd pissed himself.

Alan collapsed laughing at the new sight.

"You can't win, can you? That'll teach you for misbehaving with other men."

Alan slipped an arm around Mike's shoulder and escorted him out into the night air.

Chapter 22
BELINDA'S VISIT

Over the coming weekend, Mike had decided to invite Brett and Belinda around to his apartment for dinner on Saturday.

"I've invited Brett and Belinda for dinner on Saturday," Mike told Alan, "but I don't know whether you want to be here with them. I know you get on with Brett, but you haven't met Belinda, have you?"

"No, but I'd like to, after all, Brett knows about us together so why not Belinda."

What Alan meant about being 'together' was not that the two men were living together in the same apartment, although they did spend a great deal of time together, but they were now in a relationship, something Mike never thought would happen to him.

They went shopping together on Saturday morning to buy goods for the dinner party, and really splashed out buying bottles of wine, beer, a roast and flowers.

On arriving home, they busied themselves in the kitchen preparing for their guests, Alan peeling vegetables and Mike chilling the drinks. Both men were quite domesticated in the kitchen and both could conjure up quite a meal when they wanted to.

Later that afternoon, with the table laid and the meal on its way to being made, the two guys sat down to relax and watch a bit of TV sport.

"How much does Belinda know about us?" asked Alan.

"Well I introduced them to each other, and I'm sure that Brett's said some things to her about us, but other than that I don't know. Why?"

"I was wondering about the cocaine episode, that's all."

"I'm sure he wouldn't say anything about that in front of Belinda. I'd think he'd be professional about it," continued Mike, jumping from TV channel to channel.

The guys showered and dressed, awaiting the arrival of their guests. At 6.00p.m, Brett and Belinda arrived.

Belinda was a very plain looking girl and younger than Brett. Although she might have looked plain, she had a cheerful disposition, and could, Mike thought, make herself very attractive if she put in the effort. Alan, on seeing her thought she was quite attractive as she was, but he took to her and they settled down next to each other on the couch. Mike poured drinks and the four joked and laughed and chattered amongst one another.

"Mike, was that the first time you'd been to Berlin when you and Brett went there?" asked Belinda, sipping at her glass of white wine.

Mike smiled politely back at her. "Yes it was actually."

"And did you like it?"

Mike caught Brett's eye.

"Yes, I thought it was a great place," he replied, still smiling sweetly.

"I've never been, but I've heard it's quite an eye-opening place."

"What do you mean by that?" asked Mike.

"Well, for one, I believe there's plenty of sex there."

"I really wouldn't know about that," answered Mike, the smile now fading.

Brett spluttered on his beer and Belinda and Alan looked at the two of them.

"Went down the wrong way," coughed Brett, trying cover up his guffaw.

Belinda didn't give up.

"Have you ever been there Alan?"

"No, but I'd love to go there. It sounds such an interesting place, with all its history."

" I believe it's a haven for gays?" carried on Belinda, nonplussed.

"So I've heard," responded Alan, nonchalantly. "Maybe one day, Mike will take me there?"

"Of course," chirped Mike, "I would love to go back there."

Brett tried to change the subject to anything other than Berlin. Belinda was obviously fishing for information of some sort, but neither Brett nor Mike knew what or why.

The dinner was a success and each was surprised when they saw a little gift at their place at the table which had been placed there by Alan. After dinner, and the three men had cleared the table, all four of them adjourned to the lounge to carry on drinking and chatting.

"Mike, tell me some of the things you saw or did in Berlin," asked Belinda, not letting up on the subject of Berlin.

Brett looked nervously at Mike.

"Yes, tell us Mike," scoffed Alan, grinning at the other two men's predicament, and now siding with Belinda.

"Well we didn't have much time as it was all business," replied Mike.

"And in the evenings?" asked Alan, with an impish glint in his eyes.

Mike cast him a dirty look as if to say 'shut up!' There was a pregnant pause as Belinda waited for her answers, but they were not forthcoming.

"Weeellll?" whined Belinda.

"We sat and watched TV, had a couple of drinks and went to bed," answered Brett, in desperation.

Alan nearly choked on his drink on hearing this. Mike smacked him on the back to try to alleviate Alan's 'choking fit', and when he'd recovered, Alan came up with a suggestion of a game of charades. Belinda immediately jumped at the idea and promptly appointed the two teams.

"Mike, you and Brett against Alan and me." She grabbed Alan and pulled him closer to her on the couch. "Now simple rules," she continued, "Each side write down the titles of a film, book, play or song on a separate piece of paper, then we put ours here, in this ashtray and you have to take from there, and yours place in that vase and we'll take from there. Agreed?"

They all agreed and Mike and Brett watched as Alan brought the illustrious vase from the mantelpiece and placed it on the coffee table.

"By the way, Mike, I love your coffee table, so sturdy!" remarked Belinda.

"Oh yes," Mike giggled, "very sturdy. In fact I think it could probably take the weight of about four people it's so sturdy."

Alan gave Mike a wink and a knowing grin.

"Right are we ready? We'll go first," said Belinda. "Ladies first!"

The three men roared with laughter at this comment; maybe the drink was getting to Belinda and she was now letting her hair down.

Belinda took a piece of paper on which Mike had written down the title of a film. She looked at what was written there and then tried to enact the title. She raised two fingers.

"Two words," shouted Alan.

Belinda nodded agreement.

She raised one finger.

"First word," continued Alan.

She pointed to a ring on her finger.

"Ring?"

Belinda nodded negatively.

"Diamond?"

She shook her head, looking frustrated and pointing at the ring again.

"Gold."

"Yes," she shouted.

"You're not supposed to speak," said Brett, reprimanding her. "You're supposed to mime everything."

Two fingers were raised.

"Second word," said Alan.

Once again Belinda pointed to her finger.

"Gold ring?"

Her head shook.

She waved a finger in Alan's face in frustration. He looked quizzically.

"Finger?"

Belinda jumped up excitedly. "Yes, yes, now say it."

"Gold Finger," chimed Alan.

"Yes!" shouted Belinda.

As the game progressed, so Belinda got more drunk, but then so did the guys. There was a stage when both Belinda and Alan were rolling on the floor with laughter, their arms entwined with each other. Later, Brett and Mike were hugging each other on the success of guessing one of their charades correctly. Many a time Mike kissed Brett on the cheek when he got one of Mike's acts correct, and Belinda did likewise to Alan. At one stage, Belinda, in her drunken state, looked Alan in the eyes and slurred, "I find you verrry sexy you know!"

Poor Alan must have sobered up in an instant on hearing Belinda's comment, because the shocked look on his face sent Brett and Mike into gales of laughter.

"I do, I really do," persisted Belinda. "Don't you think he's sexy, Brett?"

Brett tried to control his laughs.

"Of course he's sexy," laughed Brett, light-heartedly to humor his girlfriend, but deep down he did find Alan sexy.

"What about you, Mike? Do you find him sexy?"

By this time Belinda had cupped Alan's face in her hands and was looking lovingly into his eyes.

"That's why I have him as my life partner, and he's not available!" exclaimed Mike, pretending to take Alan from Belinda's clutches.

"Ooh, he's sooo possessive," slurred Belinda.

The game basically broke up at this point as none of them could concentrate properly on their acting, and Brett felt it was time to take his drunken Belinda home.

"I think it's time for us to go home to bed," said Brett dragging Belinda to her feet.

She didn't catch what he'd said, but she had heard the word 'bed' and her face lit up when she said, "Are Alan and I going to bed?"

"No," said Brett, putting his arm around her to guide her to the front door. "Alan's going to bed with Mike and we're going home."

"I'll stay here with Alan and you can take Mike home with you," slurred Brenda.

The three men looked in awe at one another at the suggestion that Brenda had made.

"I don't think Mike wants to go with me, nor do I think you should go with Alan," said Brett, again trying to get Brenda towards the front door.

"Come here, my baby!" she exclaimed when her eyes caught Alan. "Give me a kiss, not an ordinary one, but one like you give Mike. Come on!"

She broke away from Brett, flung her arms around Alan and crushed him to her ample bosom. As she tried a passionate kiss on Alan's mouth, he felt a strange feeling in his groin. Was he getting a hard-on from a woman kissing him? It had to be the physical closeness of their bodies that was doing it and not the fact that it was a woman. He broke away from her clutches as fast as he was able, and moved into Mike's arms. Brett scooped Brenda into his arms, opened the front door and ushered her out into the night towards their car.

After Brett and Belinda had left, Mike and Alan crashed onto their bed and slept like babies.

Chapter 23
SWEATING IN SAUNAS

Mike and Alan woke up on Sunday morning with heavy heads, both having overindulged the night before.

"Oh, my head," groaned Alan, holding his head. "I'm never going to drink again," he moaned turning to face Mike in the bed.

They looked into each other's bleary, bloodshot eyes.

"My mouth feels like the bottom of a canary's cage."

"Well don't try kissing me," groaned Alan, hauling himself to the side of the bed and dragging himself to his feet. "A cold shower's what's needed," he mumbled, heading off to the bathroom.

Soon Mike heard the shower water running.

"What's on your agenda today?" Mike shouted to Alan.

"You won't believe it but I feel like going for a run to clear my head," came the reply.

"Well you'll have to do it on your own. I'm not in any state to be so energetic."

The water stopped running and Alan emerged from the bathroom, towel drying his hair.

"What do you feel like doing today?" asked Mike.

"I actually feel like going for a sauna and sweating all this alcohol out of my system."

"Actually, that doesn't sound like a bad idea, why don't we do that?"

"Will you come with me?" asked Alan.

"What a question! I'll come with you any time!"

Alan leapt onto Mike in the bed and the two of them began to rough-and-tumble on the bed.

"Where are we going to go?" enquired Mike.

"What about us heading to Waterloo and going to the sauna there. It will be open now."

Without a second thought, Alan and Mike showered, shaved, cleaned themselves up, dressed and caught the underground to Waterloo Station. They paid and went into the sauna. For eleven o'clock on a Sunday morning, they were surprised how many men were there already.

"Perhaps they've all come from the clubs," suggested Alan.

They stripped off and wrapped their towels around their waists and strode off to the steam room. There were three other men in there when they entered. Mike and Alan stretched out on the tiled bench and let the steam and heat exfoliate their bodies. The perspiration formed on their skin and trickled down the crevices on their bodies. They lay there listening to the dull drone of conversation coming from the other three men in the sauna. After ten minutes of intense heat and much sweating, Mike rose from the tiled bench and told Alan he was going to the Jacuzzi. Mike opened the door to the steam room and stepped out into the cooler air of the building.

The Jacuzzi was able to accommodate about eight people, and four were already feeling the bubbling water tingle against their bodies. Mike removed his towel from around his waist and stepped into the warm water. The four men already in the Jacuzzi stopped their conversation and watched as Mike, with his good looks, build and long, swaying cock, settled into the water. He lay in the water, head resting back on the edge of the Jacuzzi.

The bubbles tickled various parts of his body. He could feel jets of water beating against his ass crack, creating a wonderful sensation, while other jets massaged his back and legs. He put his head back and thought of all the things that happened to him in his life recently; the cocaine episode, the hunk, his trip to Berlin, his friend Brett, and of course his relationship with Alan. He was so happy to have Alan to care for.

"Do you often come here?" said a voice that seemed miles away.

Mike didn't really hear it. He was in his own world of thoughts. He felt a leg bump his on the movement of the swirling water. He opened his eyes to see the other four men looking at him.

"Do you come here often?" enquired one of the men.

"I'm sorry; I didn't realize you were speaking to me. No, this is my first time here, but it seems quite a pleasant place."

"We're often here," he said indicating the other three men. "We enjoy the company, and of course the sauna."

"Hmm," said Mike, not really caring how often they went to the sauna.

All four smiled at him as though he were on show. He sensed they wanted to play around, but at this particular moment, he wasn't interested. He was in his own world again.

Mike lay in the bubbling water with his eyes closed once more, dreaming. He heard someone get into the Jacuzzi and sit in the space next to him, but he never opened his eyes. His body almost vibrated from the pummeling from the jets of water. He thought of Alan and a satisfied smile started to form across his face. He felt a hand placed on his left leg. He didn't want to cause any trouble with the occupants of the Jacuzzi, so he moved his leg away from the hand, but the hand followed. He opened his eyes, ready to say something terse to the hand's owner, and he saw Alan sitting in the water next to him.

"Were you testing me?" asked Mike.

"No, why?"

Then lowering his voice to a whisper, he told Alan about the other four in the Jacuzzi. Alan looked at the tired four sitting opposite Mike and himself, then flung his arms around Mike's neck and kissed him.

"They'll probably think I'm a tart just getting into the Jacuzzi and already I've got my hands all over this beautiful man," he whispered in Mike's ear.

"Just keep at it, and then when I stand up with my hard dick, they'll have regrets for what they've lost."

The two lay in the water for some time, enjoying the bubbles and each other's company, then Alan asked Mike whether he'd ever been to this sauna. Mike told him that this was his first visit, so Alan, who had been before, told Mike about the layout of the place.

Both rose from the bubbling water, their erections alert and upright for the four others to see with envy. Alan then took Mike upstairs to an area, which had refreshments, a darkroom and rest cubicles. They sat down together and had a cool drink each; then Alan said that he was going to go back to the steam room for a while. Alan went back downstairs, leaving Mike with his cool drink. When he'd finished drinking it, he wandered around the cubicles and darkroom to see what action, if any, was taking place.

In the darkroom he noticed about five or six men stalking each other, trying to elude some and attract others of their group. A couple of the group noticed Mike and was attracted to him like flies around food. Mike felt flattered that he was so attractive to so many men, but it wasn't any of them that he wanted.

Walking between some of the cubicles, he could hear groaning coming from one of the cubicles. He stood and listened. The breathing of the men inside the cubicle was labored and heavy; the slapping of flesh against flesh was rhythmic and the groans were becoming louder. He heard a low growl followed by a cry and rapid breaths; then there was silence. He waited. The door of the cubicle opened and out stepped two young guys of about eighteen or nineteen, both sweating profusely, with their bodies glowing from the sexual exercise. Mike smiled at them as they walked past him, a knowing smile as if to say I've been there and I know the pleasure you've both experienced. He pushed down on his erection which had formed as he stood listening to the young men, and which was protruding from the front of his towel.

Mike continued around the cubicles, peering into some of them to see what was happening there. Some men were sleeping on their own, others were in conversation with a partner, and in one, was a guy fondling his balls and cock. Mike stood at the cubicle entrance and watched, fascinated. After a minute or two of watching, he ventured back downstairs to the steam room.

In the steam room, action was underway. In one corner, five men were huddled in a group, each masturbating one of the others, while elsewhere, a young guy was sucking off two cocks at the same time. Mike wandered across to the threesome and sat on the tiled bench to watch. His eyes became accustomed to the steam and dim lighting. He watched the young mouth slide along the one cock then take to the other and repeat the action. The two men were kissing each other and enjoying the luxury of someone else pleasuring them. Mike looked again and noticed that the tongue and mouth belonged to Alan. He slid from the tiled bench and went onto his knees next to Alan.

"Do you want help?" he asked, taking one of the cocks into his mouth.

"I thought you were never going to come," said Alan, spitting on the other cock to lubricate it more.

The two lovers together brought the men to their climaxes and then left the steam room.

"This is fun," remarked Mike, "sweating all our frustrations out for enjoyment. What's next?"

"I don't know about you but I think I need to cool down a bit," said Alan, heading back upstairs to the refreshment area.

Mike followed and the two sat talking to each other while cooling down.

After half an hour of cooling down and watching a multitude of people coming and going in the cubicle area, Mike turned to Alan and said, "I think it's time for you to get some pleasure."

Mike took Alan by the hand and led him to one of the vacant cubicles. They went in and lay on the plastic covered mattress that lay on the floor. They didn't close the door to their cubicle properly, so that a little light could enter into the otherwise darkened cubicle.

Alan lay on his back on the mattress while Mike lay down next to him, covering Alan's lower torso with his crotch and legs. Alan could feel the weight of his lover on him and the warm movement as Mike's cock began to increase in size. They lay there kissing each other, tongue fighting with tongue, passion melting with passion.

"I love you so much," whispered Alan, "I never want you to leave me."

"I'd never do that, Al, you mean too much to me."

Mike shuffled his position and, kneeling across Alan's legs, he moved his warm mouth down to Alan's crotch, licking and caressing his balls and cock as he did so. Alan groaned as Mike reached a sensitive spot just behind his balls and near his asshole. Mike's tongue flicked like that of a snake as it searched for its prey, until he found Alan's tight rosebud. Alan lifted his legs into the air to allow Mike easier access to his treasure. Mike licked his middle finger and gently inserted into Alan's waiting asshole, wiggling it around inside and rubbing up against his prostate. Alan's whimpers became cries of joy as Mike built him up to a climax.

The door to the cubicle opened a little more than what it had been and someone peered in. Neither Mike nor Alan was aware they were being watched because they were too preoccupied with giving each other love and pleasure. The man at the entrance quietly stepped into the cubicle, closing the door again to its previous position. He knelt down behind Mike and put his arms around Mike's waist and breathed on his neck.

Mike reacted but couldn't see the person's face in the slightly darkened cubicle, but could feel the strong arms encircling him. He felt something prod him in his back and realized it was the guy's cock. He brought his hand round to his back to feel the man's cock. He grasped it and squeezed. It was hard and long. Mike traced a finger along its length, which seemed to go on forever. Then he felt the ridge of the man's circumcised cock head. He ran his finger around its circumference and also realized that that part was also large. Throughout this examination of their visitor, Mike continued to work on Alan's pleasure.

The man pushed Mike forward so that he now leaned over Alan's cock, enabling him to take it into his mouth. The man then rubbed his engorged cock along Mike's ass crack, pushing his cock between his ass cheeks. Mike pushed back onto the hardened cock, quickening his action on Alan's shaft.

"You'd like this wouldn't you?" The man spoke for the first time.

Mike froze and stopped working on Alan's cock. He crouched there with Alan's cock in his mouth, a strange guy's cock about to penetrate him and…

"…That voice! I've heard that voice."

"Stay where you are; don't move, but enjoy this."

Mike's mind rushed into action. Where had he heard that voice? Who was this stranger?

Mike heard the tell-tale tear of foil and heard the condom being unraveled and rolled onto the waiting cock. Then he felt the coldness of the lube being applied to his waiting ass. Mike shuddered as he felt the man's thick fingers being inserted to loosen him up.

Mike felt the man's cock find his pucker. He felt the top of the huge head trying to break through and enter that one area which brought Mike insurmountable pleasure, only from some men. He was tight, so the entry was becoming difficult. He then felt three lube- coated fingers drive into his ass. He growled and released Alan's cock from his mouth. Alan opened his eyes for the first time.

"Who's here with us?" he asked Mike, almost whispering.

"Don't worry," said the stranger. "Lie back and enjoy, I want you to."

Suddenly Mike put the voice to a face.

"You!" he exclaimed, leaping off Alan and spinning round.

He felt the iron grasp of the man's hand as he was pinned to the mattress alongside Alan, while the man's other hand covered his mouth.

He also felt the breath of the man as he leaned over both of them and said, "Don't worry, I'm not here to hurt you. I need to speak to you, but first I have to give you both something you've craved."

The hunk removed his hand from Mike's mouth and his grip on him. In the dim light that reflected from outside of the cubicle, Mike and Alan could see the bulging muscles and an eagle tattooed on his arm .

"What do you want?" asked Mike in a timid voice. He knew now that his 'dream' had not been a dream, because he could feel the man's flesh, so he was real and not a ghost as they had suggested earlier.

"I want you to make love to the one you love, giving him the love he craves, and I'm going to give you the possession you crave."

"You mean…?" stammered Mike.

"Yes…," he replied, "…while you make love to you lover, I shall make love to you."

He produced a condom for Mike, tore open its foil and handed it to him.

Mike had already lubricated Alan's rosebud with his tongue, but his ass was not ready to take those magnificent nine-inches of solid, hard muscle, he needed more lubrication.

Mike rolled his condom onto his throbbing cock and, lying Alan on his side, positioned himself behind him. He gently pushed forward and Alan pushed back to meet him. He felt his cock become completely warm from the protection of Alan's ass. Once he was safely imbedded in Alan, Mike put more lubricant into his hand and greased his own ass. He felt the hunk's giant cock-head touch his asshole again, but this time, through excitement or eagerness, there was no fighting or obstruction. The hunk sank swiftly and deeply into Mike.

Mike cried out in pain as the bulbous head broke through, and held his position. No one moved until Mike murmured that he was now accustomed to the hunk's size and they could continue. He could feel the hunk's cock growing in girth inside of him and he also felt faint, exactly as he did when the hunk confronted him in the gym shower. He became afraid that he was going to pass out. The hunk started a slow rhythmic thrust and drag, and with each deep thrust into Mike, so Mike thrust into Alan. Mike was seeing stars before his eyes as the hunk sank deeper and deeper with each thrust. He could feel the man's balls slap up against his ass, just as his did likewise to Alan. Mike wrapped a hand around Alan's cock and started an upward and downward movement to coincide with each thrust. They could each feel the sweat that ran off their bodies as they slid and slipped on the wet mattress.

After what seemed like an eternity of passion, Alan was the first to cry out as he shot his load over Mike's hand. As he shot, Mike could feel the contractions around his cock tightening. He felt his balls rising up inside him and he knew that his time had come. His ass muscles clamped down tightly around the hunk's massive weapon as he fired into Alan. The hunk tried to drag out but he was clamped tightly in the warmth. Mike's ass was not letting go. The hunk's thrusts were now frantic as he unloaded his warm cum into the top of his condom and Mike felt every quiver and jolt as the hunk fired his load.

The three lay on the mattress, Mike still impaled on the hunk and Alan still impaled on

Mike; each had an arm around the other and their hot bodies slowly began to return to a sense of normality. Their breathing soon returned to normal. Mike lay there, tears in his eyes. This mysterious man had given him what he'd always wanted. The lust in him had desired this and that lust had now been satisfied.

The Hunk slowly slid out of Mike, who was sorry to lose the contact and pleasure, and sat up on an elbow and looked at Mike and Alan.

"I think that you make a fine couple and you deserve each other. My name is Bruno."

"I knew I'd heard that name before," said Mike, excitedly. "You see Alan, I wasn't dreaming, I mentioned the name Bruno. So it was you in my bedroom."

"Yes I wanted to see you to talk to you, but you were sleeping…"

"…So you climbed into bed with me instead."

"Are you sorry?" asked Bruno.

Mike looked at Alan in the dim light and replied, "No."

"How did you get into my apartment?

"You remember you had a spare key at the gym, well I took it to get in, because I didn't know whether you'd let me in."

"But why have you been following Mike and me everywhere?" asked Alan.

"I had to check up on you to see if I could trust you."

"Trust us about what?" enquired Alan.

"Trust you sufficiently to tell you something."

"So what is it you want to tell us?"

"Mike, you could be in danger, and because of your relationship, so could your lover."

"By the way Bruno, my name is Alan."

"Hi, Alan. As I was saying you could both be in danger and I needed to warn you."

"In danger from whom?" asked Mike, sitting upright on the mattress.

They decided that speaking in the cubicle might not be as safe as they thought, and that it would be better to be in the open, so they left the cubicle and went to the refreshment area, where they could see if people were listening to them.

"Do you remember a robbery many years ago in Manchester?"

"Yes," replied Mike, "but what's that got to do with you?"

"Well two of the gang were caught and imprisoned, and although many thought three were involved, there were actually five."

"Yes, I know that."

"And I suppose you know that two escaped?"

Both Alan and Mike nodded.

"I was one of those that escaped."

The two lovers looked horrified. They'd had sex with a criminal, but then was that so criminal?

Mike looked at Bruno's naked body and saw the tattoo of the eagle on his right arm.

"But two escaped," continued Mike, "and one was murdered, correct?"

"Yes, but I had nothing to do with that."

"So what was your position in the robbery, Bruno?"

"All I had to do was drive the car."

"Then who murdered the fifth guy?" asked Alan, getting himself another cool drink.

"That's where the danger comes in."

"Why?"

"Why do you think the robbery took place?" asked Bruno.

They both shook their heads.

"Drugs! It was a break-in to steal millions of pounds worth of drugs to sell on the black market."

Mike and Alan took in everything that Bruno told them about the drugs, the robbery and his position in it, but never once did he mention the names of the other robbers. He then explained why both of them had seen him in so many different places, because he wanted to make contact with them to tell his story and warn them. He had also noticed how the two guys had been eyeing each other and presumed that they would be in a relationship.

"The next question we need to ask," said Mike, "is do we go to the police about this or not?"

"That's another reason why I wanted to make contact with you, Mike, was because of your friend Brett, who's a cop. I thought that he could do some private investigations without having the entire police force running after me."

"So do we tell him or not?" asked Alan.

"Not for the time being," pleaded Bruno, "there's some other business I need to clear up before you call him in, so I need to go."

"When can I see you again?" asked Mike, "there are other things I need to know."

"I'll be in touch, but in the meantime, say nothing and be careful."

He looked at the clock on the wall in the refreshments area, saw the time and gave his apologies and made his way to the showers and head off into the night.

Bruno was gone leaving Mike and Alan possibly more bewildered than ever. At least one mystery had been solved that night – which person was the mystery hunk.

Chapter 24
REVELATIONS

The following day, Mike was at work when a phone call came through for him, it was Bruno. He told Mike, the minute that he picked up the phone, not to mention his name during their conversation, in case someone in the gym heard him speaking to Bruno. He asked whether Mike was going to be at home alone later that afternoon, because if he was, Bruno wanted to come around and speak to him. Mike agreed to take off from work early and go home, but Bruno had told him not to do that as it might look suspicious to some people, but he didn't elaborate and say which people.

At approximately four o'clock, Mike said that he had a doctor's appointment and needed to go off. As doctors don't consult after five or six o'clock, he was able to leave. He dashed home and waited for Bruno.

Thoughts were running through his mind, knowing that he and Bruno would be alone together; would he be able to control his hormones with this hunk sitting in the same room as him? He quickly tidied up the apartment and waited for the doorbell to ring.

At five minutes to five, it did. Mike raced to the door and opened it to find Bruno standing there. Bruno entered quickly so that no one would notice him, then they went into the lounge, where Bruno removed his dark glasses. Mike offered Bruno a drink but he declined the offer.

Once inside the lounge and comfortably seated, they started to chat.

Mike asked Bruno if he knew anything about some cocaine being left under a vase in Mike's apartment, but Bruno said that he wasn't aware of it, yet had a suspicion as to who might have placed it there and why.

"Who?" asked Mike.

"Steven," came the reply.

Mike was stunned.

"Do you know Steven?" he asked.

"Oh yes, very well," replied Bruno, standing and crossing to the window. He stared vacantly out of the window and quietly said, "He's the trouble."

Close up and in the daylight, Mike could see the rugged beauty in Bruno's face; the taut muscles straining against the flimsy cotton of his T-shirt, and the bulge in the front of the jeans, showing Bruno's manhood stretching down the left leg while his hefty balls occupied the space in the right leg. In a way, Bruno reminded Mike of Geoff, large, bulky and domineering and he liked all three characteristics.

The doorbell rang out two short, sharp rings. Bruno stopped in mid-sentence and looked startled.

"Who knew I would be here?" he immediately asked.

"No one. I didn't tell a soul, not even Alan. Stay where you are and I'll see who it is."

Mike got up from his seat and ventured towards the door.

"Who is it?" he called.

"Brett," came the reply.

Mike thought that it might be good for Brett to hear Bruno's story, but he wasn't sure how Bruno would take to talking to a cop. Bruno heard Brett's name and became agitated.

"Go into the bedroom and I'll try to get rid of him," said Mike, seeing Bruno's consternation.

Mike opened the door and stood in the doorway.

"Hi Brett, how are things?"

"Fine. I thought I'd pop round to see how you were and find out if you'd heard anything more about our mysteries."

Mike hesitated at the doorway.

"Everything's fine, thanks Brett," he said, giving a nervous laugh.

Brett sensed that something wasn't quite right and tried to leer into the apartment, but Mike blocked his view.

"Are you sure everything's okay?"

"Yes. No problems," came the nervous response.

"Have you got someone here?"

Mike began to panic. Had Brett seen Bruno?

"No," stammered Mike.

"Are you having a scene with someone and you don't want Alan to know?"

Mike didn't like that suggestion because if he said 'yes', he wasn't sure whether Alan would find out from Brett later.

"No!"

"Mike, are you in trouble?"

The word 'trouble' echoed through his head. It was the same word that Bruno had used when referring to Steven. Brett could see in Mike's eyes that something was troubling him, so he changed his tactic.

"Do you mind if I come in and get a glass of water, please Mike; I'm dying of thirst."

He knew that obliging, kind Mike wouldn't refuse that request. Mike hesitated, then relinquished, hoping that Bruno was safely ensconced in the bedroom.

"Sure, I'll get it for you."

He left Brett standing in the doorway and headed quickly to the kitchen to get the water.

While he was gone, Brett ventured into the apartment and looked around the lounge. There on the marble coffee table he spotted a pair of dark glasses, which he'd never seen before. Mike returned with the glass of water and gave it to Brett. Brett drank slowly from the glass, savoring each taste of the water and delaying his departure. As Brett drank, so he tried to take in the whole lounge to see if there were any other telltale signs. He finished his water and handed the glass back to Mike, who escorted him to the front door. Brett turned to face Mike at the threshold.

"Mike, what's going on here?"

"I told you, nothing, now please go."

Brett decided he was not leaving his friend so easily. He spun on his heels and headed towards the main bedroom with Mike scampering behind him, trying to prevent him from entering there. Brett walked into the bedroom to come face-to-face with Bruno. They stared at each other.

"I'm sorry Bruno," said Mike, looking crestfallen. "Brett, let me introduce you to Bruno. Bruno, this is Brett."

The two men shook hands, while glaring into each other's face.

"Are you the one who's been haunting Mike?" asked Brett rather brusquely.

"If you put it that way, yes, but I had a reason."

"And I'd be very interested to hear that reason," said Brett, adopting his police tone.

Rather than arguing in the bedroom, Mike suggested they return to the lounge and discuss the whole affair like adults.

"Why don't you start at the beginning and spill the beans," remarked Brett, still maintaining his air of authority.

Bruno started to unfold the story. He had been part of the robbery in Manchester in which a large quantity of drugs was stolen. Yes he had escaped capture, but no, he'd not killed anyone, nor had he been directly involved in the actual robbery. He was only the driver.

"What happened when you first confronted Mike?" Brett asked.

"He saw me in the shower and I think at first it was a physical attraction between us, but then I realized that perhaps I could trust this guy and confide in him. I needed to have someone that I could speak to."

"What did you do to him to make him pass out?"

"Absolutely nothing."

"I think it was the excitement," replied Mike, coming to Bruno's defense.

"And in Alan's case?" asked Brett.

"Again I don't know, maybe it's my magnetic personality," joked Bruno.

"What about Berlin?" Brett questioned. "Why were you there?"

"That's where the murder took place and I followed to see if you were investigating that and whether you were onto my case."

"Who committed the murder?" enquired Brett.

At this stage, Bruno hesitated and seemed awkward at revealing the name of the person.

"I can't help you if you don't help me, Bruno," said Brett, producing some compassion in his voice.

Brett rose and wandered over to the window. The shadows were lengthening outside and the brightness of the setting sun was diminishing.

"Please help us Bruno," pleaded Mike. "If you help us, I'm sure that Brett will help you, not so Brett?"

"That's a promise. If we get an arrest, you can always turn state witness and perhaps, for your support, we could cut a deal," replied Brett.

Bruno still stood looking out of the window, listening to their suggestions. Eventually, he turned and faced the other two.

"Sam Baxter."

"Who?" asked Mike, sounding confused by this new name.

"Sam Baxter was the guy who committed the murder in Germany."

"And who is Sam Baxter?" enquired Brett.

"When he returned to England, he changed his name," continued Bruno. "You know him as Steven Bass."

It was as though Mike had been slammed in the midriff by a ten-ton truck. The gasp that emanated from him was audible. Both Brett and Mike looked absolutely stunned by this information. Bruno moved back to his seat and watched the two friends. Nobody spoke for a moment. Mike's mind was now racing; the cocaine, Steven's visit to his apartment, his sarcasm at work, it all began to add up.

"But why me?" Mike asked.

"I'm sorry, Mike, that was my fault. He saw me at the gym, and as you know I'm not a member. I had to sneak in, in order to try to make contact with someone. He saw me one day, recognized me and asked me what I was doing there. I used your name, as it was the only one I'd heard and told him that I was a friend of yours. Will you forgive me for that?"

Mike gave a brief smile and a nod of the head.

"So do you think he planted the cocaine in my apartment and why?" queried Mike.

"Probably hoping to get you arrested and out of the way in case you knew too much about him."

Brett sat listening intently to all that Bruno had to say. He had to admit things were now falling into place and he believed what Bruno was telling them, but they had to have a plan to get Steven.

A shrill ringing sound was heard and Brett pulled his mobile phone from his pocket. He answered, listened patiently then switched off his phone. He looked at Mike, who could see from Brett's expression, that something was amiss.

"Mike, Alan's been shot."

"What!" shouted Mike, jumping from his seated position and grasping Brett by the shirt.

"What are you saying? When? Where is he?"

Words were flowing from Mike, wanting answers. Brett took hold of his friend firmly by the shoulders and shook him, trying to calm him down.

"Mike, Mike, calm down. Alan's fine, he's alive. It was only a flesh wound and he's in hospital, but he's fine, I promise you."

"I've got to get to him," screamed Mike, tears rolling down his cheeks.

"Just relax, I'm going to take you to him. Bruno, I think you'd better go with us, as well. I need to question you some more and I think you might be safer with us."

Mike grabbed his apartment keys and all three headed for the hospital.

Chapter 25
THE SHOOTING

At the hospital, Mike ran on ahead of the other two to the information desk to find out where Alan was. He was given the private ward number and he hurried ahead, Brett and Bruno in hot pursuit. Alan was lying in his bed, eyes closed, naked from the waist up. Around his left shoulder and arm was a bandage. Mike went to his bedside, leant over his lover's body and kissed him gently on the forehead. Alan didn't open his eyes. Mike stood there, tears welling up into his eyes. He felt helpless. He wanted to take Alan in his arms and hug him and make everything well again, but he knew he couldn't. Bruno and Brett stood on the other side of the bed.

"Alan, can you hear me?" called Mike softly.

There was no response.

"They've probably drugged him," said Brett, looking at the drip going into Alan's right arm.

Mike moved closer to Alan so that their lips almost touched. His warm breath fell onto Alan's mouth, and then he let his lips rest gently on Alan's. He didn't exactly kiss him, but rather just rested them there. Alan's eyes flickered open. Mike moved his face away from Alan's so that he could see those beautiful eyes again.

"Hi honey, are you all right?"

Alan smiled on recognizing the face. Mike took his right hand and held it, squeezing it to show his love. Alan slowly became more aware of his surroundings and the people who were there. He smiled at them all, including Bruno.

"Hi, there buddy," said Brett, revealing a face full of relief that Alan was alive.

Alan once again smiled and greeted Bruno by name.

As Alan became more conversant, he was able to tell them what had happened.

He had packed up for the day at the office and was preparing to go round to Mike's apartment. He had caught the lift downstairs with four other colleagues and they had chatted merrily while on their journey. When he reached the ground floor, he and another woman from the office walked out of the building together, he to go in one direction and she in another. He had probably walked about ten meters when he heard what he thought was a car backfiring. He felt an intense pain in his left shoulder and collapsed onto the pavement, but as he did so, he managed to see in the car that was parked outside the offices, the person with the gun. After that, he remembered nothing. He assumed that someone must have called an ambulance and that was why he was now in hospital.

"Did you recognize the person in the car?" asked Brett.

Alan lost his gentle smile and a serious look appeared on his face. He turned to Mike, squeezed his hand and in a quiet voice, barely audible said, "Steven."

"Now we've got him for something else," said Brett excitedly. "Are you one hundred percent sure that it was him, Alan?"

"Absolutely! Why?"

Brett moved away from the bed, took out his mobile phone and dialed his superior.

Another half an hour was spent visiting Alan explaining what Bruno had told them about Steven, and then the nurse arrived to chase them along. "You can always come back tomorrow."

"I'm sorry, nurse, but we're not leaving yet. I'm a police officer," said Brett, showing his identification, "and I've just phoned through for someone to stay on duty outside the ward door. This patient has to be kept under police safety while he remains here. When the police guard arrives, we'll leave."

The nurse was quite happy to accommodate this situation, so the guys stayed longer; trying to cheer Alan up until the police guard arrived.

When they eventually left, Brett told Mike not to leave his apartment and to phone in sick the next day. He didn't want Mike going to the gym and if Steven was there, for them to have a go at each other.

"Stay out of his way," said Brett, "he's dangerous. Bruno I think you must do the same."

"Do you want to stay at my place, Bruno?" asked Mike.

"That would be nice, thank you."

"Take us both back to my place, and we'll stay there until you feel it's safe for us to go out," Mike told Brett, as the three got into Brett's car.

Brett dropped them outside Mike's apartment and waited for the two men to go inside before departing.

Inside the apartment, Mike offered Bruno something to drink, which he accepted, and the two men sat in the lounge discussing the day's events and what they could do. At one o'clock in the morning, Mike and Bruno were still trying to concoct plans to get Steven.

"I don't know about you, but I'm ready for bed," said Mike eventually, stretching and yawning. "I'll make up the bed in the spare room for you Bruno."

"Thanks Mike. I appreciate your kindness."

Mike quickly made up a spare bed in the second bedroom; bade Bruno a good night and went off to his own bed. He stripped off and fell on top of the bed covers, in the dark, except for the streetlights shining through the open curtains. His mind flashed back to Alan lying wounded in the hospital. Why hadn't he been there for his lover? Why had Bruno come into their lives? All this could have been avoided if Bruno hadn't appeared on the scene! He lay there thinking it all Bruno's fault. As he was thinking, he saw a silhouette standing at the entrance to his room. It was Bruno.

"Mike, are you still awake?"

"Yes," came the soft reply.

"May I come in?"

"Sure."

Bruno moved to the foot of the bed. In the streetlight, Mike could see that he was also naked.

"I've been lying in bed thinking and I just wanted to say how sincerely sorry I am about all this and what's happened to Alan. I never knew it would get to this stage where people were going to be hurt, and especially people who have been good to me."

"Bruno, I know deep down inside of me that although I keep blaming you for getting us involved, I don't blame you for what has happened to Alan. That was not your fault."

"If I could do anything to make it up to you two guys, I would."

"You can do something for me now, if you like."

"Sure, what?"

"Bruno, would you mind lying on the bed next to me? Just hold me, please."

Without saying another word, Bruno came round to the side of the bed and lay down next to Mike. He put an arm across Mike's chest and pulled him closer. The two men now lay in each other's arms, and fell asleep.

When the two of them awoke, they were still entangled in each other's arms except they both had erections.

Bruno opened his eyes first and looked down at their throbbing cocks dueling with each other, and smiled. Mike then opened his eyes and saw Bruno watching him.

"Hi there. Thanks for staying over last night, I really appreciated it, buddy," said the soft dreamy voice.

Bruno let his hand drift down to Mike's swollen cock, gave it a hard squeeze, winked and said, "My pleasure."

Mike trailed a finger over the scar above Bruno's left eye. "How did this happen?"

"A little mishap with Steven Bass, but you really do not want to know about that."

At that, the subject was dropped.

Mike phoned the hospital first thing that morning to enquire how Alan was doing, and was told the usual line of "he's had a good night's rest." Other than that, they said nothing. He then phoned Brett to find out what was going to be done and was told to stay put in his apartment and not even go to the hospital.

"But what about Alan? I've got to see him."

"Not today, Mike. I can tell you that Alan's in the best hands, other than yours of course, but he's under police guard, so you've nothing to worry about. I'll phone you later."

"What's the verdict?" asked Bruno, after Mike had switched off the phone.

"We've got to stay here Brett says, but Alan's okay."

Mike felt almost like Alan, a prisoner in his own home, not being allowed out, but if Alan's safety had been in jeopardy, then so could Mike's.

Mike switched on the television to see if there had been any mention of the shooting, but nothing was mentioned.

Neither he nor Bruno had bothered to get dressed after their naked sleep, so they wandered around the apartment au natural. Mike was able to take in every aspect of Bruno's body in the greatest detail.

"You've got a magnificent body, Bruno; such symmetry and definition. No wonder you give me such a hard-on when I see you."

"But you also have a great body, Mike, and it's your tight ass that gives me my hard-on," replied Bruno, grinning an impish smile at Mike.

"Now look what you're doing, " said Mike pointing to his crotch. His cock was bobbing in the air, growing longer and harder. His foreskin slowly began to roll back, revealing his pink head.

"I dig watching your foreskin do that," said Bruno, rubbing the palm of his hand across his circumcised head.

After an hour's lovemaking, the two sweaty bodies collapsed in a heap on the floor and there they lay until their breathing had returned to normality.

"You always give me great satisfaction when you're inside of me, you know, Bruno. From the first time I saw you, there was something that attracted me to you, but it's not the same attraction as I have for Alan."

"I know, it's lust," replied Bruno. "You lust after my body as others lust after yours. Haven't you noticed how people are attracted to your body?"

"Yes, actually I have."

"Well, all you're doing is the same to me. You lust for my muscular body. In your mind I am more of a man and you want to be dominated by someone who, in your opinion, is more manly than you, if I could put it like that."

"When you put it like that, I suppose you're right, but I can't help it."

"You don't have to worry, we all have our fantasies and desires. The only difference between you and me is that I like to dominate and you like it both ways, depending on the other person's needs."

"Have you ever let anyone get into you?" asked Mike, rather hesitantly.

Bruno gave a wry smile. "Are you trying?"

Mike became flustered by this answer.

"No."

"Well, maybe if you try harder, you might, one day."

At lunchtime, Mike's mobile phone rang. It was Brett on the line.

"I've got good news for you, Mike, Steven's been arrested."

"Where?"

"In Leamington Spa. We put out an all bulletins call and he was spotted in Leamington Spa by some cops who happened to be off duty and on holiday."

"That's great, Brett, but what about Bruno? What's going to happen to him?"

"I told you, he's going to turn state's witness and we'll do a deal. He'll be fine, I promise you."

"Where's Steven now?" asked Mike.

"The cops are bringing him back now, he'll probably be at the police station by about 5.00 p.m, if you'd like to come down here."

"I'd like that very much, to get my hands on that bastard."

"Now, now we won't have any of that, otherwise you'll be in trouble."

Mike was about to hang up when he heard Brett add something else.

"Oh, by the way, I was also asked to tell you that you could fetch Alan. He's allowed to go home."

There was a loud scream and a cheer as Mike switched off his phone.

"Alan's coming home," he shouted, leaping around the lounge and hugging Bruno. Then as an after thought, he added, "The police caught Steven in Leamington Spa."

"Thank God for that," sighed Bruno. "You don't know what a relief that means to me, now that he's been caught after all these years."

"They should have him at Brett's police station by about 5.00 p.m. so we can go and pick up Alan and then go down to the police station, if you'd like."

The two men got dressed and headed off to the hospital, both with an air of confidence and a spring in their step.

Chapter 26
CAPTURED

At the hospital, Alan was ready and waiting for Mike to fetch him. He had on a dressing gown over his bare shoulders and a pair of jeans, when Mike and Bruno arrived.

"Wow, who's looking sexy without a top on? Are you baring that sexy midriff for the benefit of the nurses?"

"No, for you," was the immediate response.

"Well, I'm glad to see that you haven't lost your sense of humor!"

"Did Brett contact you?" asked Alan.

"Yes, that's where we're going now. He said that they were bringing Steven back to his station at about five o'clock."

Bruno helped Alan into the front seat, while he got into the back. All the way to the police station, he watched Mike's happy, animated face in the rear-view mirror. Once or twice Mike caught his eye and winked and gave Bruno that knowing smile.

At the police station, Brett was waiting for them. They went into his office and he found some extra chairs for them. The mood was frothy and light-hearted. They were all laughing and joking while they awaited Steven's arrival.

"You said that he was caught by some off duty cops," said Mike; "thank goodness they were alert to have recognized him."

"It was a good thing that they were there, because they're not our guys. None of ours were there at the time."

Almost to the minute, the lead car, followed by the escort car arrived with the prisoner. The car stopped outside the entrance and Steven was taken from the car, handcuffed.

"Alan, I want you to remain in my office, but would you guys mind leaving for a moment, please. We need Alan to make a positive ID of the suspect. Once that's been done, then we can bring you back in."

Mike and Bruno went into an adjourning room to wait to be called back in, while Alan sat and waited.

The door to Brett's office opened and Steven was led in. Alan's eyes met Steven's and they glared at each other like two animals ready to fight.

"Sit!" said Brett sternly to Steven. Then, turning to Alan he said, "Have you seen this man before?"

"Yes," came the brusque reply.

"Was this the man you saw shoot you?"

"Yes, sir," came the reply.

"Thank you. Take him away and lock him up."

As they escorted Steven away, Brett shouted, "Could you send the policemen who captured the accused, into my office, please?"

Alan sat calmly now that Steven had formally been arrested and was being locked away. Mike and Bruno both came back in.

"Did you see him?" asked Alan.

"Only being taken down a corridor," answered Mike.

Just then the door to Brett's office opened and the arresting policemen entered.

"You required us, Inspector?" said the one, standing very erect.

Mike looked at them, then his jaw dropped open and a gasp was emitted.

"I don't believe this! Alan, look!"

There in front of them stood Sergeants Geoff Aston and Pavel Hanak.

The four friends greeted each once more and were extremely glad to see one another.

"What's this sergeant business?" asked Mike, bubbling with excitement.

"We're both in police forces. I'm in the Los Angeles Police Department and Pavel is stationed in Germany," said Geoff, throwing an arm around Mike's shoulder.

"But I thought Pavel was from the Czech Republic?" said Alan.

"I was born there and lived there all my life, but three years ago I moved to Germany and joined the police there. However, when I do bodybuilding competitions, I represent the Czech Republic."

It was so good to see their two guests that they almost forgot about Bruno and Brett, who were standing transfixed by this show of emotion and affection between the four. Mike suddenly realized that they were ignoring Brett and Bruno.

"Hell, I'm rude. I didn't even introduce you. Pavel and Geoff let me introduce you to Brett, a very good and old friend of ours, and Bruno, a very good and new friend of ours. Bruno, you know what I mentioned earlier to you back at our apartment, about what you did to me, well these two guys do the same, but with them I get double the quantity."

On hearing this last line, Mike, Alan, Geoff and Pavel roared with laughter, while Brett and Bruno looked a little bewildered.

"Must be an in joke, Bruno," said Brett, shaking his head in disbelief at their antics.

Mike nudged Bruno with his elbow and said, "I'll tell you later why we're laughing," then looking at the others, he continued and said, "Perhaps we might even show you later!"

"Geoff," said Alan cautiously, "there is something I need to ask you. When I saw you scratching through our bedside drawer and you told me you were looking for condoms, what were you looking for?"

Geoff appeared a little embarrassed by this question.

"I was actually looking for drugs. You see, although Pavel and I were taking part in the bodybuilding competition, it was also a cover. We, the DEA in America, had been given a tip-off about drugs being sold and distributed from a gym, and as the murder had taken place in Germany, it meant that the German police were brought in. That meant that Pavel and I had to work together, which, by the way was great fun. We knew that Mike worked in a gym and we'd heard that cocaine had been planted in your apartment and so we were looking for it, but you found it first and destroyed it. We wanted to see if there was any more lying about, and that's when you caught me. But, having said that, we also had run out of condoms and there was no way that Pavel or I was going to have sex without one."

"I'm glad to hear that," said Mike. "Tell me Pavel, if you're in the German police force, have you ever heard of a guy by the name of Thomas?"

Pavel laughed. "Oh yes, he's my superior. In fact it was he who suggested that I take the case because he'd already met you and he thought you and I might, how you say, have something in common!"

Mike and Alan grinned and gave each other a knowing wink, and then Mike said, "This calls for a party. We've all got to get together and celebrate the end of this dramatic line of events and the coming together of our friends."

"I like the coming together bit," remarked Geoff.

"But I'm afraid there's going to be one proviso…" continued Mike.

"… And what's that?" asked Alan.

"This is a man's world so only men are allowed. Sorry Brett."

"What do you mean, sorry?" Brett questioned. "I'm a man."

"Yes, but can you take it like a man?" sneered Mike. "It's men only, no wives or girlfriends!"

"So what's the problem?"

"What we mean is that Brenda can't come to the party; it's only for us guys."

"No problem, and I'll show you what a man I can be," replied Brett.

The other guys laughed and joked with Brett, suggesting that his ass could be in danger if he came to the party.

Chapter 27

LEATHER SHOPPING

Alan moved in with Mike over the next few days and his injury healed well. They had decided that Alan needed caring for, so it would be easier if he was to move into Mike's apartment and leave mother's furnishings behind. In Steven's absence, while he awaited trial, it was decided at the gym, to put Mike in charge until a new manager could be appointed and Mike was thrilled with his new temporary position of acting manager.

Mike had been in contact with their friends and had arranged the promised party. They were going to have it over the weekend, starting on Friday and if the guys could cope and wanted to, they could continue over the entire weekend, so if they wanted to stay over, they'd better bring extra clothes, if they felt the need to wear clothes. There was also one proviso for the party, which Mike had stipulated – no jeans to be worn; only the barest of clothes, such as shorts of any type of material or posing briefs. Of course the guests could arrive dressed 'normally', but once they entered the apartment, they would be obliged to disrobe and wear their party outfit. All the guys thought this a crazy but great idea; even Brett went along with the idea, but insisted that Belinda not be told about the dress code.

"Why on earth not?" asked Mike over the telephone.

"I don't want her getting ideas," was the rather ridiculous response from Brett.

"That you might be gay?" asked Mike.

"Well, if you put it that way, yes," he hesitantly replied.

"Honey, you like men as much as you like women, so she'd better get used to the idea if you're ever going to marry her. In any case, with this glorious summer that we're enjoying, what's wrong in wearing shorts?"

"Mike, when you go to work on Friday, will you drop me in town so that I can do some shopping?" asked Alan.

"Sure, but will you manage with your shoulder?" queried Mike.

"Yeah, I'm sure I will, and in any case I need to get it fit and ready for the weekend."

"Why what are you planning on doing?" came a quizzical voice.

"Wait and see," was the stoical reply.

FRIDAY: the day of the party arrived.

Mike and Alan left early for the center of London, so that Mike could unlock the gym and Alan could go and do his shopping. As it was still too early for the shops to be open, Alan waited at the gym with Mike. He sat in the refreshment area watching muscles straining, biceps bulging and an accompaniment of groans, grunts and heavy breathing coming from the early morning enthusiasts.

"Any one would think these guys were having orgasms with all that grunting," commented Alan to Mike.

Mike smiled at this comment and agreed with Alan.

"These are the quiet ones," said Mike. "Wait until the heavies move in, then the earth feels as though it's shaking."

Mike busied himself with some of his early morning clients while Alan continued to gaze in wonder and awe at some of the bodybuilders. These early morning guys were generally the genuine bodybuilders, not like the afternoon people who were there mainly to get fit and be seen; but not necessarily in that order. Alan also realized for the first time that he had never actually sat and watched Mike at his work, because if Alan had come to the gym, he had done his training while Mike was usually busy with someone else.

Alan sat bemused and intrigued at the way Mike handled some of his clients. The ones who were there to do serious business, Mike worked well with, but the lazy scene setters were treated almost nonchalantly with a certain amount of disdain. Alan could see that Mike knew his work and what was required of him, and he thought that Mike could make a very competent manager, if he applied for the position. At 8.00 a.m, when Mike had finished with his last client, he joined Alan in the refreshment area.

"You know something, I'm impressed by the way you do your job, or are you just doing it for my benefit?" said Alan.

"Why thank you, kind sir, and what are you after with such flattery?"

"Oh nothing in particular."

"So why the flattery?"

"Because you deserve it," came the serious answer. "I am genuinely impressed with you, and in my honest opinion, I think you should apply for that bastard Steven's job. You'd certainly do a far better job than him."

"Do you honestly think so, Alan?"

"I wouldn't say so if I didn't think that you'd make a good job of running this place, and I'm sure you'd like to make it your own, wouldn't you?"

"You're right, I would."

"By the way, Mike, do you know whether any drugs have been sold from here?"

"You mean him dealing? I don't know, perhaps Brett might do some investigations here."

Alan looked at his watch, saw the time and decided to head off to do his shopping. He bade Mike goodbye, said he would see him back at the apartment and set off. As Alan was in the Holborn area, he decided to take a trip to Great Eastern Street. He caught the underground, alighted at Old City underground and then walked to his destination, his favorite leather shop.

He entered the doorway and descended the steps into the shop with the smell of leather permeating everywhere. He walked around looking at the various leather and rubber items on sale as well as the various accoutrements. He saw some whips and shuddered. He didn't fancy being beaten with those, not even by Mike. He loved the feel of leather, but he wasn't into any masochistic fun.

"Can I help you, sir?" asked a tall, sturdy shop assistant.

"Yeah, I'm looking for a pair of leather or rubber shorts."

"Size?"

Alan looked at the assistant and gave a wicked grin. "Seven inches!"

The assistant blushed.

"I'm sorry, sir, I meant what size shorts were you looking for?"

Again Alan gave one of those wicked grins of his; of course he knew what the assistant was getting at, but he decided to have some fun with him because he was quite good looking in his leathers and with a shaven head.

"I'm actually not sure," replied Alan. "It depends on the cut. It's either a size 32 or 30."

"Would you follow me, sir, and I'll show you what we've got then you can try them on."

They wandered over to a number of shelves filled with leather and rubber shorts. They looked for the two sizes that Alan had mentioned, pulled a couple of samples from the shelves and the sales man held them up for Alan to scrutinize. Alan looked at them, and then decided he didn't really like the rubber ones so he ditched them.

"I think we'll stick to leather."

He found three different designs, some with pockets, others without; some with a button fly, others with a zip fly.

"Let's try these," he said to the assistant, selecting two pairs of shorts.

"If you come this way, sir, you can try them on."

The assistant led Alan to the change rooms. It was a fairly small area with a full-length mirror against the wall, and a door. The assistant showed Alan in, handed him the clothes, said that he would be able to assist in any way should Alan require, and then closed the door, leaving Alan to try on his shorts.

Alan slipped off his jeans and briefs, because he loved the soft feel of the leather against his skin. He stepped into the first pair, the size 32 and pulled them up. He buttoned up the fly and then looked at himself in the mirror.

"Hmmm! Not bad," he said, turning around and viewing his tight ass, "but I'm not sure."

He opened the cubicle door and looked out hoping to catch the assistant's eye, which he eventually did. He waved to the assistant who came hurriedly to the cubicle.

"What do you think?" asked Alan, turning around for the salesman to see.

"Very nice, sir."

"Are you talking about the shorts or the ass?" asked Alan, giving his little grin.

"If you don't mind me saying," said the salesman, in a hushed tone, "both, sir."

Alan smiled broadly.

"Thank you, but truthfully, what do you think?"

"Why not try the other one and see?"

Before the salesman had a chance to exit from the cubicle, Alan had pulled down the button shorts and was standing half naked.

"Please close the door, before people see me," said Alan, trying to sound concerned about his nudity.

The salesman obliged and the door was shut, with both of them now inside the cubicle.

The salesman looked into the mirror and could see Alan's flaccid cock hanging below his balls and swaying gently with his movement. The salesman's eyes never left the mirror and his view. He could feel the leather constricting his cock as it began to enlarge. His cock was growing bigger by the minute and he was unable to control its movement as he stared at Alan's cock in the mirror. Alan bent over to step out of the one pair and into the other. As he did so, he felt the hard muscle pushing up against his bare ass. He held his position for a moment, enjoying the cold leather against him, and then he pulled up the second pair and, smiling at the salesman in the mirror, zipped up the fly.

Alan could see the swollen cock outlined in the salesman's jeans, and he felt the start of his own erection. He stood facing the mirror as his cock grew in length. When it was protruding almost horizontally, except for the leather constraint, he turned to face the salesman.

"How do you think these look?"

The salesman could hardly speak. His throat was dry, but his cock was wet. Keeping his eyes fixed on the salesman's face, Alan slid a hand over the hard, engorged penis that took up most of the front of the salesman's jeans. Alan gripped the length and squeezed; it felt a good length. The salesman became almost weak in Alan's hands.

"What do you like doing?" whispered Alan into the salesman's ear.

"Anything," came a very breathy reply.

"Do you want to suck my dick?" asked Alan, sounding very threatening.

"Yes please," quivered the dry voice.

In a flash, the man was on his knees, paying homage to Alan's bobbing cock. The man obviously had plenty of experience, because he handled Alan's cock with such passionate expertise, that Alan wasn't able to contain himself and came very quickly, shooting into the man's face and chest. Alan looked down at the man's head, which never stopped moving along Alan's throbbing cock even after Alan had been exhausted of every last drop of semen and the head of his cock was now becoming sensitive. Eventually the salesman rose to his feet, smiled politely at Alan and said, "That was great, thank you."

"No, it's I who must say thank you. Nobody's ever made me come so quickly before. You sure know how to use your mouth."

Again the salesman smiled, sheepishly. Alan took a handkerchief from his pocket and wiped the man's hair and chest to remove all signs of his cum, put the handkerchief back in his jeans pocket on the floor and said, "Which pair do you like?"

"The zip fly ones," came the reply.

"Fine, I'll take them."

Glowing warmly from his leather shopping, Alan took his parcel, which included other small items, thanked the salesman with a friendly smile and caught the underground back into the center of the city. He headed for Soho to Old Compton Street, where he was gong to have some lunch. While there, he bumped into a couple of his friends and sat and chattered to them, while watching the passing trade, and then wandered off to catch the underground back to Mike's apartment.

Chapter 28

THE PARTY

Back at the apartment, Alan unpacked his shopping, put drinks in the fridge to chill and then went and had a shower. After showering, he started preparing a variety of hors d'oeuvres for the party. Once those were completed, he cleaned the apartment and put some flowers in the now famous vase in the lounge for decoration and color. He then scattered condoms and lube around the apartment, like one might scatter cushions, also for decoration – after all, one didn't know what this party might produce with six horny, virile young men let loose on each other. He then wrapped little gifts, that he had picked up on his shopping spree, for the guests.

Mike arrived home from work a little early in order to help with the preparations for the party. When he walked in and saw what Alan had done he was not only impressed, but humored by the ideas that he'd come up with.

"What are these?" he asked, pointing to the small gifts.

"Oh just a little something for everyone," replied Alan.

"What are they?"

"You'll see when the others arrive and everyone opens their gift. You never know, they could come in handy," he remarked with an impish smile.

Mike just shook his head and laughed, knowing the fun-loving Alan. He loved to see Alan happy and enjoying himself, and he felt that they had become much closer to each other as a result of all the incidents which had befallen them.

"Come and sit here with me for a moment," said Mike indicating the couch.

The two of them sat down together.

"What's the problem?" asked Alan.

"No problem, I just wanted to say thank you for everything; everything you've done for me and everything you mean to me. Your love makes everyday-living turn into something meaningful and each little thing you do becomes something special. I sometimes don't think you'll ever know how much you mean to me, and when I thought I might lose you through the shooting, I was devastated. I never really thought I'd meet someone special with whom I could settle down and have a relationship with, but I think I was wrong, because I have you and I want you to know, that whatever happens tonight, I love you."

"What do you mean, whatever happens tonight?"

"Things might happen when we've had a few drinks that we don't expect; people might come onto us for example, but I want you to know that I'm yours forever."

"I love you too, Mike, and I know what you mean, so you've got nothing to worry about."

"Right, now that's out of the way, how was your day?"

"Very busy – shopping, shopping and more shopping; oh and eating lunch and getting an outfit for tonight."

Mike's eyes lit up.

"What outfit?"

"You'll have to wait and see, but the man who sold it to me was very nice."

Mike giggled at Alan. "Very nice, or verrrry nice?"

Alan took on the face of a naughty boy and said, "verrrry nice."

"I'm glad to hear that, there's nothing worse than an unhelpful salesman."

"No, he was verrrry helpful, you might say."

Both men collapsed into peals of laughter as Alan proceeded to tell Mike of his visit to the leather shop and how helpful the salesman was.

Mike went and showered in preparation for the evening's party, while Alan changed into his outfit. When Mike walked into the bedroom, towel draped around him, he was astounded to see Alan standing there with a leather harness across his bare chest and his new sexy little leather shorts.

"Wow, you look sexy! Did you buy those today?"

"Yeah, do you like them?"

"I reckon I could get into those and what's in them," he said, flinging his towel from his body and rubbing his wet torso hard against Alan. "I know somebody who's going to get it tonight, looking like that."

Alan gave a slight smile and then very seriously said to Mike, "Who?"

Mike tackled him and flung him onto the bed.

"Ow! My shoulder," shouted Alan. "I need to be handled gently, remember."

The two lay there glued to each other's lips and in a tight embrace, only to be broken by the ringing of the doorbell.

Mike leapt up from the bed, quickly pulled on a pair of shorts and headed to the door. The first of their guests had arrived; it was Bruno. He stood at the door in a pair of tight cut off jeans turned into shorts, his bulky thighs bulging to break free from the denim constraints, and a white T-shirt.

"Come in Bruno, said Mike ushering the young man into the lounge. "Make yourself at home; you're the first to arrive but the others shouldn't be long."

Bruno flung himself into an easy chair while Mike went to the kitchen to get a drink. Alan came into the lounge and greeted Bruno.

"How are you feeling, Alan?" asked Bruno pointing to Alan's already healing wound.

"I'm fine thanks," was his reply.

"You're also looking very sexy," continued Bruno.

"Thanks, but what are you after," joked Alan.

"That slim, trim body of yours," said Bruno, winking at him.

Alan blushed a little at the compliment, as Mike returned with drinks for the three of them.

Mike then excused himself while he ran off back to the bedroom to get dressed, returning a little later in a white string vest and white Lycra shorts which emphasized the large bulge that he carried in his crotch.

The three sat chatting about the upcoming trial of Steven's and wondering what the outcome would be, when the doorbell rang once again. This time it was Geoff and Pavel.

They entered the lounge and Alan noticed that both were also wearing white string vests like Mike's, which emphasized their muscular chests, more so Geoff's because of the darkness of his skin coloring, and each had on a pair of sweat pants.

"I thought Mike said no jeans or longs," shouted Alan. "It had to be shorts. You two are cheating."

"Oh, don't you believe it; we wouldn't let you down, Alan. Check this out," said Geoff pulling his sweat pants down to his ankles and stepping out of them. He stood there in his white vest and the tiniest of gold satin posing briefs. Alan's eyes lit up and a grin formed from ear to ear.

"Wow!" he exclaimed. "That's wicked!"

"Now what have you got to say?" asked Geoff, encouraging Pavel to remove his sweat pants as well.

Pavel, very seductively and slowly, almost as in a strip show, began to slide his sweat pants down over his hips, revealing a flat stomach. They continued their journey and soon the guys were facing a pale blue pair of satin posing briefs, which bulged as it strained to retain its contents. Pavel stepped from his sweatpants and turned around for all to admire.

"Well, what do you think?" he asked his audience.

"How the hell do you fit that huge package of yours into that small piece of material," asked Mike, admiring the young man's truly incredible physique.

"I tie it in a knot," laughed Pavel, as he ran a hand over his crotch.

The only guest still outstanding was Brett, but Mike knew that he wouldn't be long in arriving. About fifteen minutes after the two undercover cops had arrived, Brett turned up. As he stood in the doorway, Mike admitted to himself that he was a bit disappointed by Brett's attire.

"You look as if you've just come from a soccer match, buddy," he said.

"Don't be misled. Maybe I have just come from soccer."

Brett was ushered into the lounge and offered a drink.

"Are those the only shorts you could find? They don't look very sexy," remarked Alan pointing to Brett's white soccer shorts.

"It's not the shorts that are the important part," responded Brett, "It's what's underneath."

"So what is underneath?" enquired Alan.

"Ah, you'll have to wait for that," taunted Brett, pulling one of the legs of the shorts up his thigh, but not revealing what he had underneath.

Snacks were offered and the drinks flowed freely. There was much chatter and friendly banter amongst the six of them, mainly about the arrest of Steven and his up-coming trial. Finally, Alan decided it was time for them to eat, before they became too drunk. He ushered them all to the table, which had been laid out beautifully. The table groaned under the weight of the food that had been prepared for the guests.

"This is self-service. Take what you want, find a place to sit and enjoy, but before you do that, there's a small gift for each of you with my thanks for what you all did for me," said Alan. "The gifts are all wrapped in identical paper and no name tags are on them, so you simply choose a gift and it's yours. There is, however one small catch to this; you have to open your gift before you start eating."

The five other men each chose a beautifully wrapped box and started to open their gifts. As each person opened his box, there were gales of laughter. Geoff opened his to find a pair of handcuffs; Pavel's contained a set of nipple clamps; Mike's had a silver metal cock-ring, which pleased Alan; Bruno's was filled with a dildo and Brett's contained a leather whip. The men couldn't get over their gifts and continued to laugh about it well into the meal.

"What's the idea of these?" enquired Pavel.

"The idea," said Alan "is that if later in the evening you have the urge to do something fun, you can use your gift to enhance that fun."

Brett flicked his whip in the air and asked what Alan thought Belinda might say about it.

"That's up to you, whether you want to tell her and show her, but I think she might be using it on you."

Mike was excited about his gift and asked Alan to assist him with his metal cock-ring, so they went into the bedroom and once it had been positioned around his balls and cock, he raced off to the bathroom to look in the mirror. On his return to the lounge he flaunted his gently hardening cock and balls to the others, much to their enjoyment.

"But you don't have a gift," said Mike, suddenly realizing that Alan had nothing.

"Oh, but I have; four wonderful friends, one lover and a hot pair of leather shorts. Now eat!"

After their meal was completed, Mike and Brett cleared the plates away while the others scattered themselves around the lounge. Pavel and Bruno were sitting in a corner on the floor, totally involved in each other's conversation, while Alan and Geoff were looking out of the lounge window, admiring the twinkling lights.

Geoff's hand slid down Alan's back and over his rounded butt in its leather casing. He squeezed it gently at first and whispered, "You look very sexy in this outfit, Alan. I dig this tight ass of yours."

Alan never rebutted Geoff's touch; instead, he tensed his ass-cheeks tightly.

"Mmm! That's nice and hard."

From the corner, Pavel and Bruno watched as Geoff's hand slid over the two mounds of leather. Still Alan remained stationary at the window.

Mike and Brett re-entered the lounge after clearing the plates and dishes away. Brett sat on the couch while Mike crossed to where Alan and Geoff were standing. Mike stood next to Alan, on his left, while Geoff remained on Alan's right.

"Are you touching up my boyfriend?" asked Mike, casually across to Geoff, with a grin on his face.

Geoff never removed his hand when Mike said this, but smiled a knowing smile to Mike. Mike wasn't slow in joining Geoff feel the smoothness of Alan's ass. Occasionally, their hands touched, but they continued stroking Alan.

Geoff's gold satin posing pouch was beginning to extend in the front, trying desperately to contain its weighty contents. Mike glanced down and noticed the ever-increasing golden bulge on Geoff, and immediately he noticed his own hardening shaft throb in his Lycra shorts. Alan allowed the two men to pleasure him and arouse each other.

Bruno and Pavel, not to be left out of anything, got up from the floor and crossed to the trio. Pavel stood behind Mike, put his arms around him and pressed his heavy crotch up against Mike's bubble-butt, while Bruno knelt in front of Geoff and kissed the gold covered bulging mound as it continued to grow.

In the meantime, Brett watched intently from the couch, rubbing his hand over his silk-covered crotch. He watched for a while as the "outsider" and then couldn't contain himself any longer. He pulled his soccer shorts to the floor and revealed a shiny, canary yellow Speedo with his erection straining at the material to escape; in fact his long, hardened cock was outlined under the material and the tip of his circumcised cock peeked over the top of his costume. He walked round the group and positioned himself in front of Alan. He kissed Alan's soft lips, letting his stiff cock rub against Alan's and then trailed his mouth down over Alan's nipple, over the ripped abdomen, until his mouth reached the throbbing leather crotch. Throughout all this, no-one spoke, but people communicated with their eyes, hands and bodies.

While Mike felt Pavel's groin slide over his ass-crack, he turned his head to meet Pavel's lips and Mike felt his foreskin roll back, freeing his cock head. At the same time, Alan turned his head to meet Geoff's tongue, waiting to be sucked upon.

Bruno pulled Geoff's pouch down to allow his throbbing dick to break free of its constriction. The circumcised head bobbed in front of his mouth and pre-cum oozed from his piss-slit. A wet tongue licked under its length, sliding upwards until it reached the tip, then engulfed the entire head, sucking up the love juice.

At the same time, Brett undid Alan's shorts, unzipped them and pulled them to the ground. The naked torso appeared appealingly before him. He smiled up at Alan and glanced his tongue over the waiting cock head. As he did this, with his free hand he stretched across to Bruno kneeling beside him and felt for his cock in his jeans. He felt the swollen cock trying to break free, so he obliged by unzipping Bruno's jeans and hooking his cock out with his hand and pumping it while he continued to lather Alan's pulsating manhood.

Mike broke his kiss with Pavel, watched as Brett lapped along Alan's manhood, and put a hand behind him to rub along the length of Pavel's erect cock, which had forced itself above the elasticized waistband of his pouch. Mike felt the warm flesh protruding from the top of the pouch. He pushed his hand over its length, and as he did so, so Pavel shucked Mike's Lycra shorts to the floor. With total freedom Mike pushed his ass-cheeks back against Pavel's hard weapon, at the same time watching Brett sink his mouth slowly down the length of Alan's cock. The silence of the room was now being intermittently broken by groans and gasps from the men, as they explored each other.

Alan eventually moved away from the group, taking Mike and Geoff with him. He lay on his side on the carpet in the center of the lounge. Pavel, Brett and Bruno soon followed and the six became an entangled mass of writhing bodies on the floor, with wandering hands and searching mouths.

Geoff stretched out and found a condom on the coffee table, tore open the foil and unrolled the sheath over his bourgeoning cock. He found some lube and began to lubricate Alan's waiting asshole. As he did so, Brett continued to worship Alan's throbbing cock, lapping up the escaping love juice from its tip.

Mike slid Pavel over onto his back, reached for a condom and, placing it at the tip of Pavel's bargepole, he placed his mouth over the top and proceeded to push the condom slowly down the length of Pavel's massive rod with his mouth. As he did so, so Pavel's foreskin unraveled to reveal a glistening, wet cock-head. Mike then took the lube, and inserting two fingers into his own asshole, he lubricated himself. Having prepared himself, Mike slowly sank his twitching rosebud onto Pavel's cock. Mike's sphincter clamped tightly shut, grasping Pavel's stem, as he felt the slow penetration, but Mike didn't need to get used to this large weapon, he desperately wanted it so he simply sank on it until his butt cheeks rested on Pavel's balls and pelvis, and then he gave a long, slow groan of pleasure.

As Mike rested there for a moment, Bruno moved across Pavel's chest so that he faced Mike. As he bent over to suck on Mike's pulsating cock, his butt cheeks flared apart near Pavel's face. Pavel held the cheeks apart with his hands and began to rim Bruno's waiting hole.

With each touch of the tongue, Bruno's rosebud reacted and a gentle sigh was heard from him. Pavel's tongue dug deeper into the waiting entrance, lapping up the muskiness and causing Bruno's cock to throb.

Geoff's grunts became louder as his hard, deep thrusts bore into Alan and his body began to glisten with sweat. As Alan's body jerked from Geoff's thrusts, so Brett's mouth fought to retain Alan's cock. Brett had removed his Speedo and was rapidly pounding his own meat. Geoff grabbed Alan's nipples and squeezed them hard. He felt Alan's ass muscles clamp tightly around him as he did so. Throughout, no-one spoke or gave commands, only the slapping of flesh on flesh and the grunts of excited men was heard.

The first to come was Brett, who let go of Alan's swollen cock as he shot onto the floor, gasping. Geoff watched Brett fire his load and continued his relentless pounding of Alan's ass, bringing himself closer to his climax. His grunts were louder now and sounded animalistic as his thrusts became desperate. He cried out loudly, took hold of Alan's hips for support and immersed his full length into the warm regions of Alan's body. Geoff's body went rigid and with each load that was fired, Geoff pushed deeper into Alan until slowly his rigidity began to relax and his breathing returned to normal.

Adjacent to them, Mike was riding Pavel's bargepole like he was riding a horse. He would rise to its tip and just before Pavel's cock would slip out, Mike would clamp his ass muscles and drop his body back onto the solid weapon.

Alan felt desperate to come and so he moved to the three still busy on the floor. Bruno had rolled off Pavel's chest and Alan knelt down and placed a condom on Bruno's solid rock. Alan, on his hands and knees, bent over Pavel and placed his lips on Pavel's, kissing him intensely; in doing so he raised his ass for the taking. Bruno did not hesitate. Bruno spread both cheeks and inserted his tongue. He tasted the remainder of the lube and muskiness of Alan's ass, which inflamed his desire to penetrate Alan's waiting butt-hole. Firmly gripping his enlarged cock, he guided his weapon towards the waiting entrance. Slowly he sank his cock head into the pulsating hole. He watched as the mushroom-shaped head disappeared from view and he could feel that although Geoff had been inside Alan, Alan's warm cavity had not become loose, but still maintained its tightness. Bruno watched as he slowly sank his shaft deeper into the waiting cavity until his balls lay tight against Alan's butt. He held his position for a moment and felt his cock throb in its confines, and then he began the slow retreat until the whole stem was visible and only the head remained hidden from view. He began to pull the head out, but he could see Alan's sphincter tighten around his shaft, disallowing exit. Again, he pushed slowly down immersing his cock into the warm interior of pleasure. As Bruno increased his speed and pumped in and out, he took hold of Alan's dribbling cock and started to stroke him. His hand slid easily up and down the full length, aided by Alan's quantity of pre-cum which lubricated his cock. After some time, both men began thrusting against each other and both Alan and Bruno knew they were nearing the end of their journey. They erupted simultaneously. Bruno held tightly onto Alan's warm body until he began to relax, then slowly he began his withdrawal, but Alan's tight ass fought to prevent this from happening.

"Keep it there. Don't take it out yet," pleaded Alan, being the first to speak. He wanted to luxuriate in his pleasures.

Bruno obliged willingly as he felt content with his cock firmly entrenched in this fine sturdy ass. Finally, he and Alan collapsed together on the floor in each other's arms.

The four men sat watching while Mike and Pavel continued to make passionate love to each other, writhing and rolling on the floor; one minute Mike was riding Pavel, and the next, Mike was on his back, muscular legs thrust in the air, being penetrated. The four men watched intently, fondling with their own and each other's slowly diminishing erections, trying to maintain their uprightness. Of the four, Bruno's cock remained erect and the more he manipulated it, the harder it was getting again.

They all moved in closer to Mike and Pavel, almost like a pack of hyenas waiting for the kill. Their hands caressed Mike and Pavel's naked bodies, as well as their own. Alan bent over Mike and kissed him, forcing his tongue into his lover's mouth. Geoff pinched both Pavel's nipples, causing him to thrust even deeper, while Bruno encased Mike's cock in his warm mouth at the same time as Brett guided Bruno's already throbbing cock into his mouth. Brett could taste Bruno's salty cum that had remained after he had removed his condom and enjoyed its flavor. All six men became part of the build up to Mike and Pavel's eruption.

Mike's prostate was taking a pounding from Pavel's bargepole and both bodies were aglow with sweat. Mike's pecs became enlarged and his nipples hardened while his breathing was becoming heavier and he could feel his balls rising in his sac. Bruno pulled on Mike's ball sac, squeezing them as he did so. Mike's eruption was nearing. Pavel sensed this and increased his speed and intensity, submerging his nine-inches plus deeply into Mike's waiting asshole, slapping his balls against Mike's butt hole as he did so.

"Fuck!!" screamed Mike, breaking free from Alan's kisses. "Harder!!" He pleaded. "I'm going to come!"

Pavel obliged with increased intensity, his muscular arms gripping onto Mike for support and grunting loudly as each thrust became harder as he pulled all the way out and then rammed back in. The more intense they became, the more the other four increased their actions.

As Mike cried out, Bruno released his mouth from Mike's cock which exploded, splaying jism over his chest, stomach and Bruno's face, and causing his ass muscles to strangle Pavel's pounding rod. Pavel couldn't contain himself any more. As he was about to shoot, he withdrew from Mike, ripped off the condom, and, leaning between Mike's legs and covering Mike's body with his own, he pounded his cock in a frenzy. His body vibrated and shook as shot after shot rose from his balls and white cum flew across Mike's stomach and chest, there to mingle with Mike's own. It seemed as though this was a never ending stream of jism. Mike's chest and stomach were spattered with white and when he was spent, Pavel lowered his body onto Mike's and let their breathing and sweaty bodies mingle as one.

The air reeked of sex as the six friends slowly relaxed and allowed themselves the luxury of sleep to overcome them.

Chapter 29

NIGHT ESCAPADES

The stillness of the night loomed over London and Mike's apartment. Sleep came easy to the exhausted and alcohol-filled young men. It had been decided, prior to the party, that there would be no specific sleeping arrangements. In short, where you collapsed, you slept.

Naked bodies were scattered everywhere, with only Brett opting to sleep on a bed in the spare room. Alan had chosen the couch, while the others lay in an easy chair and on the carpet in the lounge. No one had ventured into the main bedroom.

The night crept on and the silence was only broken by the occasional snore. The traffic outside seemed to have come to a halt and peace reigned in the home. An odd grunt or groan could be heard, but other than that there was stillness. Outside the city lights twinkled and the glow lit up the apartment, while the river continued its silent flow.

At an early hour Geoff woke up with a cramp in his thigh, so he got up off the floor to stretch the thigh muscle. Once the cramp had subsided, he went quietly off to the bathroom to have a piss. Pavel, who lay awake, watched him as he made his way though the darkened room. Pavel had woken up with a hard-on and he felt he needed that taken care of.

Pavel waited a while then followed Geoff to the bathroom. When he reached the door, he saw Geoff sitting on the toilet seat, sliding his hand along his enlarged cock. Pavel watched for a while, and then moved forward. The large silhouette entered the bathroom. Geoff looked up but carried on with his task. Pavel stood between Geoff's legs and, taking hold of his erect cock in one hand, began to sway it in front of Geoff's face. His cock slapped Geoff across the left cheek, and then he did the same across the right cheek. Geoff, with his left hand, grabbed hold of it, pushed Pavel's foreskin back and slurped his now naked cock head straight into his mouth. The sudden warmth sent a quiver down Pavel's spine. He slowly started to thrust the remainder of his cock down Geoff's throat until Geoff's chin came to rest against Pavel's balls.

Geoff noticed Pavel's nipple-clamps, which he'd earlier left in the bathroom. He reached for them and stretching up, clamped then on Pavel's nipples.

"Aagh!" came a breathy gasp as the metal clamped hard on each nipple. As that happened, so Pavel's cock jerked, throbbed, and was thrust forward deeply.

"I'm going to fuck you," he hissed quietly.

Pavel pulled Geoff to his feet, opened the glass shower door and stepped in, taking Geoff with him. He pushed Geoff against one of the walls of the shower and forced his mouth onto Geoff's. This was rough passion, as the two muscular bodies pushed against each other. Their lips crushed against each other's like two animals head-butting each other, and their tongues fought a battle for control, but Pavel's firm grip kept Geoff pinned to the wall. Pavel thrust his pelvis forward, rubbing his engorged length against Geoff's. Geoff thrust back to meet the onslaught. Pavel lifted Geoff's arms in the air and licked under his cleanly shaven armpits. He could taste the sweet manliness of Geoff's sweat and this made Pavel all the lustier. Geoff groaned as Pavel moved his mouth over Geoff's bulging biceps and licked them too. Each time that Pavel did this, his pelvis gave a hard thrust.

Brett happened to wander into the bathroom to relieve his bladder, and saw the two cops entangled together in the shower. He stood transfixed as they continued to thrust at each other. He fondled with his slowly growing cock, stroking it in time to each thrust. Pavel saw him and gestured that Brett should join them in the shower, but before doing so, Pavel asked Brett to get Geoff's handcuffs from the lounge. Brett quietly did as he was requested and soon returned to the shower with the handcuffs. Pavel positioned Geoff so that his thick arms were held up and he handcuffed him to the shower nozzle which hung over the center of the shower. Geoff's chest muscles stretched as his arms reached skywards, his dark brown nipples protruding from his light brown skin, and his stomach muscles flattening. Brett moved to Geoff's front and started to work on his dick, salivating all over it. While he did this, Pavel nipped out of the shower and fetched a couple of condoms and some lube. When he returned, he handed Brett a condom and whispered to him, "Get that on buddy. I want you to fuck the hell out of him."

Even in the limited light that flowed in from the outside, one could see the delight on Brett's face. He unrolled the condom, lubricated Geoff's ass and positioned himself behind Geoff. His hand felt for the magic entrance between the two globular mounds of ass flesh, and finding it, shifted his cock in that direction. He pushed gently at Geoff's asshole, but Geoff wanted no gentleness. He suddenly pushed back hard, impaling himself on Brett's cock. The feeling of pleasure that hit Brett forced him against the side wall and he gasped as he felt the tightness of the warm ass snugly cover his dick. So intense was this feeling that Brett thought that he would instantly blow his top. In fact, he had never experienced such a formidable attack on his erect cock before, not by anyone, including Belinda.

"Fuck him!" hissed Pavel standing in front of Geoff. Pavel gently licked at Geoff's nipples, nipping at them and running his tongue over the two mounds. He took off his nipple clamps and placed them on Geoff's hardening nipples. Geoff growled like an angry lion, and pushed back harder, forcing Brett's cock deeper into Geoff's bowels. Pavel pinched the clamps tighter, causing Geoff to puff out his chest and grind on Brett's cock. This action was nothing Brett had ever experienced and as a result, he held on to Geoff's hips to try to control the frenzied action. Brett continued ploughing into Geoff's firm ass, sliding in and out with gritty determination. He could feel himself getting closer to shooting. Again, Pavel clamped hard on the nipple clamps and again Geoff's chest thrust out and he ground his ass against Brett's balls and stomach. The more intense the pain, the more Geoff enjoyed the moment. The pre-cum was oozing from Geoff's cock and glistened in the dim light, with each deep thrust of Brett's penetrating cock.

Pavel continued to squeeze the nipple clamps sending streams of pleasurable pain running through Geoff's body, and with each squeeze came a throb from Geoff's cock which often rubbed up against Pavel's own flailing hard-on.

"Aagh! I'm going to come," hissed Brett.

Pavel put his arms around Geoff to steady him while Brett pummeled into Geoff's ass. Pavel could feel Geoff's cock rub up against his own and felt the wet pre-cum spread over his length. As Brett fired his full load, Geoff could feel Brett's cock throbbing with every spasm, and he continued to grind. Eventually, Brett's pumping action slowed down and when he was spent, he withdrew his subsiding penis from its warm hideaway. He took off the condom and threw it into the toilet bowl.

"Stand in front of Geoff and do as I tell you," commanded Pavel.

"No," came a voice from the dark. "I've watched you cops at it, and it's time for someone else to show you. Brett you can go and relax if you like."

All their heads turned to the voice. Mike stood there with his cock-ring still maintaining his hard-on, his cock fully sheathed in a condom and lubed, ready for action.

"Then take Brett's place," said Pavel.

Brett exited the shower and watched as Mike moved to being in front of Geoff, while Pavel moved to behind Geoff and slowly inserted his hefty cock into Geoff's waiting ass. The thickness of his cock expanded the entrance to the cave of warmth, causing Geoff to cry out in pain, but it was more a pleasurable feeling than a painful one. Pavel sank deeper and deeper in the realms of Geoff's tight ass, while Geoff, getting used to Pavel's size, pressed back onto the bargepole.

"Pinch his nipples with those nipple clamps, but hard," commanded Pavel.

Mike squeezed hard on the clamps and Geoff cried out with pleasure, grinding his ass up against Pavel's cock and stomach. The more Mike pinched, the more Geoff ground. Pavel gasped as he felt the tightness of Geoff's ass muscles around the stem of his cock. He held onto Geoff's waist and encouraged him by pulling him closer towards him, thus thrusting even deeper into Geoff. This action was turning Pavel on. He could feel his cock being squeezed and twisted inside Geoff's warm ass, as he drove into Geoff.

Geoff was swinging from his handcuffs as he pushed and twisted his ass against the bargepole, which was easing its way in and out of his aching ass. Mike leant forward and savagely bit on Geoff's lips and savored the taste of his mouth. Their tongues fought for control, and as they did so, Mike could feel Geoff's heavy breathing on his mouth and face. It was now Mike's turn to feel the wetness of Geoff's cock sliding up against his own sheathed cock.

Pavel continued to pound into Geoff until his cock could take no more of the grinding and twisting. Pavel gave a low groan and his rigid body told Mike that his load was being emptied into the condom, which Geoff's ass held so tightly. Even when Pavel had fired his load, Geoff continued to grind his firm bubble-butt up against Pavel's stomach, not wanting Pavel to withdraw.

Pavel eventually slowly withdrew his cock and said to Mike, "You go for it buddy, this ass is yours now. We've loosened him up for you." He also exited the shower and stood with Brett to watch the action.

Mike walked behind Geoff and instead of inserting his cock he turned on the shower so that a gentle shower of warm water fell over their bodies. Geoff gasped on feeling the water over his tired body, but it invigorated his body at the same time. Mike slipped in where Pavel had slipped out and took over the pounding. Mike could feel the ease with which he entered Geoff, knowing that Geoff's ass had been well and truly lubed, yet even though two men had "loosened" up Geoff's ass, his ass was still tight around Mike's cock. Again, Geoff treated Mike to his grinding movement, which soon had Mike crying in ecstasy. It felt as though Geoff had at his disposal a vice-like grip, which brought sheer joy to the guys fucking him. Mike couldn't explain how this man was able to create this feeling of tightness, but he could and he sure knew how to please a man's cock. Mike felt as if his cock were being sucked into Geoff's ass without him having to push it in. It felt exactly like someone sucking on it, except there was no mouth doing the work. Mike had never experienced this feeling from anyone before and thought it might be something to do with his muscularity.

Mike clamped his arms around Geoff's chest and pulled the cop closer to him, burying his cock deeper inside of the young man and both men glistened from the water as it gently splashed over them. Throughout this, Pavel and Brett continued to rub their burgeoning cocks, sliding their hands over each other's body.

Mike's fingers felt for the hard nipples clamped by their metal constraints and he squeezed. The more he squeezed, the tighter the grip on his cock. This vice-like grip was like heaven to him and it was getting him closer to his climax.

Mike whispered softly into Geoff's right ear, "You're one helluva fuck, buddy, but you're getting me close."

On hearing this, Geoff's thrusts became more intense and he gasped, "Go for it Mike; I'm going to shoot as well. Pump me hard and squeeze me."

Mike did exactly that. Both men cried out together, and Pavel moved back into the shower and knelt in front of Geoff and watched as his two friends' bodies vibrated together, his cock throbbing as he watched their action, while Brett moved in behind Pavel.

Pavel took Geoff's wet and throbbing cock in his mouth and waited for him to shoot his load, while he continued to masturbate himself. Brett leaned over Pavel's kneeling body and placed his mouth on Geoff's and their tongues searched each other's mouth as he pumped his own cock. As the water flowed, so did their love juices. The sounds that emanated from the shower were drowned only by the splashing of the water onto the shower floor. Finally when they had no cum left, both Geoff and Mike breathed heavily but neither wanted their passion to end. Mike continued to give Geoff gentle thrusts of his now subsiding cock, while Geoff continued to push back on Mike's cock, not wanting him to pull out and Pavel continued to kiss Geoff's diminishing cock, while Brett continued to gently kiss Geoff's lips. Eventually, Mike slid gently from the warmth of Geoff's firm ass and pulled off his laden condom and threw it in the toilet.

The shower water continued to rain down upon the four men, washing their bodies and invigorating them. Mike unlocked Geoff's handcuffs and the American slumped into Mike's strong arms, where he held him for some time; they then dried themselves and, accompanied by Brett and Pavel, Mike and Geoff quietly made their way to the main bedroom where the four of them curled up in each other's arms on the bed together, and fell into a wondrous sleep.

While they had been busy in the bathroom, Alan had lain awake listening to the sounds emanating from there. He lay on the couch, playing with his swollen cock and rolling his balls in his hand, but had decided not to join the others in the bathroom. Instead, he slid from the couch and moved onto the carpet where Bruno lay, his well-muscled body, naked.

Bruno's breathing was settled as he was deep in sleep, but Alan moved in closer and blew cool air gently onto Bruno's thick cock which lay casually across his left leg. Slowly, his cock came to life and twitched. As Alan continued to blow air gently over the full nine-inches, so it grew both in length and girth. Alan noticed Bruno's gift of the dildo lying on the coffee table. He stretched across and picked it up. It was a good ten-inches in length and almost equally thick in circumference. He returned to blowing cool air on Bruno's cock while he lubricated the length of the dildo.

Bruno sighed and adjusted his position so that he turned onto his side. Alan froze and waited to see whether Bruno would wake up. After a moment, the muscular chest rose and fell as the breathing returned to its previous pattern. Alan slid beside Bruno and, lubricating his finger, slowly inserted it into Bruno's pulsing ass-hole. Bruno never moved, but his cock seemed to get harder.

After a while, Alan removed his finger and replaced it with the tip of the dildo. In the dim light, he watched with anticipation as he slowly inched the dildo deeper and deeper into Bruno's hole. Both Alan's and Bruno's cocks were rock hard and pre-cum was leaking from both their cocks, but Bruno remained unperturbed. Alan continued the journey of the dildo into Bruno's depths until he felt it could go no further; then just as slowly, he began to drag it out again. Just as he was about to pull the dildo right out of Bruno, Bruno groaned and rolled onto his back, forcing the dildo back into his cavity. His legs were splayed enabling Alan to move between them.

Alan's mouth moved to Bruno's cock-head, taking in the sweet syrup which was oozing from the piss-slit with his tongue. He then slowly pushed a few inches of man-muscle into his throat. At the same time, he gently began a rhythmic action of push and pull of the dildo as it traveled in and out of Bruno's man-hole. As Alan pulled the dildo out, he could feel the strength with which Bruno's ass muscles fought to prevent its escape.

As Alan lay between Bruno's legs, sucking his cock, Bruno lifted his legs, making his hole more accessible to the dildo. Alan stopped sucking on Bruno's cock and watched as the sphincter muscles clamped tightly around the dildo. Alan then slid a finger into Bruno's ass at the same time as the dildo entering. Bruno emitted a low groan and Alan felt him push down on his finger and the dildo. Alan slid his finger out and replaced it with two fingers, along with the dildo. He felt Bruno's chute stretch to a new limit and again felt the pressure of Bruno pushing down onto his fingers. This time, Alan kept his fingers firmly embedded in Bruno's ass as he slid the dildo in and out. There was an abundance of salty-sweet syrup leaking from the tip of Bruno's throbbing cock and Alan was feasting on it. He felt Bruno place a hand on Alan's head, encouraging him to suck him deeper and faster. Alan took the hint from Bruno and increased not only his actions, but that of the dildo. He felt Bruno insert two fingers alongside his and the dildo. This action turned Alan on and caused him to increase his speed. Alan devoured Bruno's cock and buried it deep in his throat.

"Fuck me!" sighed Bruno, forcing the dildo deeper into his cavity and encouraging Alan to quicken his action. Alan's head moved rapidly up and down the length of Bruno's cock until he felt it increase in size and felt the first shots of warm salty cum hit the back of his throat. He sucked and swallowed as fast as he was able, but Bruno's load was plentiful. The more the dildo and their fingers probed Bruno's cavity, the more cum flowed into Alan's waiting mouth, and spilled out, until eventually, he could taste no more syrup coming from Bruno.

Slowly Bruno lowered his legs, but maintaining the dildo deep in his ass.

"Sit on me so that I can pleasure you," said Bruno quietly.

Alan lifted himself and sat on Bruno's still hard cock. Although it was no longer rock hard, Alan could feel the warmth and length that lay between his ass crack. As he sat astride Bruno's crotch, Bruno started to slide his hand along the length of Alan's wet cock and thrust upwards at the same time. Alan needed no lubrication because he had produced enough as he satisfied Bruno.

It didn't take long for Bruno to bring Alan to the edge of no return, and Alan fired the first of a number of shots onto Bruno's chest and stomach. As Bruno pumped Alan's shaft, so his cum acted as extra lubricant allowing his hand to slide smoothly over its length. When Alan's supply was exhausted, he leaned across Bruno's stomach and chest, kissed the young man gently and embraced him until they both fell asleep again.

Chapter 30

THE COURT CASE

Neither Mike nor Alan had ever experienced such a bonding weekend as that which they had just completed. They felt that their own bonding had been strengthened, by the visit of their friends and they also felt that their relationship was made all the more strong by the fact that they had enjoyed each other's company without showing any of the signs of jealousy.

Mike was glad that the six of them had got together, because he felt that it had built a lasting friendship between them, and they were now really close buddies. Even Brett didn't seem as distant as he sometimes did, especially when Belinda's name was raised.

Mike knew that although Pavel and Geoff would return to their respective countries, they would always remain close and in constant touch. As for Bruno, he was now part of the 'family', as far as both Mike and Alan were concerned; after all it was this man who had indirectly brought them together.

They all had something in common. They had a desire for the male body; were gay, even Brett was beginning to doubt his bisexuality, when he said that men gave better blowjobs than women and were nicer to fuck; they were friends and they were bodybuilders, some more serious than others.

The day of the trial soon arrived and Steven was taken from his cell to the court. As had been suggested earlier, Bruno turned States Witness, giving evidence against Steven, a.k.a Sam Baxter.

The courtroom was crammed with the curious and the not so curious and those whose job it was to be there. The charges were laid before the accused and he was asked to plead. Naturally, he pleaded not guilty.

Throughout the trial, Steven's eyes never left Bruno or Mike. It was as though he held them totally responsible for his predicament.

When Bruno was called to the stand, he told the court how, on the day of the robbery, he'd been the driver of the get-away car and that the other four had been the ones who stole the drugs. He also told of how they, when they were on the run, split up and he, Steven and the murdered man had skipped the country and headed for Germany. It was soon after their departure from England that the other two men were captured, tried and were currently serving their prison sentence.

Bruno went on to tell of how they stayed in Berlin, living fairly comfortable lives, mainly from the sale of the drugs.

"When did the murder take place?" asked the prosecution.

Bruno explained that there had been building tensions because Steven wanted the money from the sale of the drugs for himself, and that the murdered man had confronted Steven one night in their house in which they were staying. An argument ensued and Steven had stabbed the man. The stabbed man had fallen to the floor whereupon Steven proceeded to kick him in the body.

"Did you try to intervene and stop him?" asked the judge.

Bruno said that he had, but because Steven had himself been under the influence of drugs at the time, the steroids that he was on gave him super strength and Steven had knocked Bruno unconscious, causing a cut above his left eye which had left a scar..

Bruno continued that when he regained consciousness, the stabbed man was lying in a pool of blood and was dead and Steven had fled. Bruno said that it was he who had actually contacted the police, but had not given his name for fear that he might be implicated in the murder.

Questions were asked back and forth, especially by Steven's defense, in an effort to disprove Bruno's statements but Bruno held his ground. The defense even tried to lay the blame at Bruno's feet saying that in their opinion, he could very well have committed the murder himself, but still Bruno didn't falter.

The following day the court proceedings couldn't take place as Steven had been hospitalized with suspected food poisoning. Everyone wondered whether he in fact had tried to poison himself or was trying an escape ploy. He was taken to hospital and placed under police guard.

"I want to go to the hospital and see that bastard," Mike said to Brett.

"Don't be a fool. You could be charged for interfering with the suspect and in any case, what do you want to see him for?"

"To find out why he shot Alan."

"Leave it," emphasized Brett, "it'll come out in the trial."

Mike chose to ignore Brett's advice and made his way to the hospital. He didn't actually know what he'd do if he saw Steven. When he arrived there he asked at information where Steven's ward was. The sister on duty asked whether he was family or a member of the police. Mike wasn't sure whether to say police or family because they might ask for proof, so instead he said, "He's my boss and I need to know what's to happen at work while he's away."

The sister considered this a legitimate request and conceded and so Mike made his way down the corridor towards the ward. As he neared the ward, he saw a young police officer sitting guard outside the ward. When Mike approached him the young man stood up and asked Mike if he could help him.

"I wondered if I could go in and see Steven?" asked Mike.

"I'm afraid not, sir," said the handsome, young officer, "unless of course you're family."

"I explained to the sister on duty that he's my boss and I need to know what is going to happen to the business while he's here in hospital," continued Mike.

The young policeman looked at Mike suspiciously. Mike knew that he wasn't going to get into that ward very easily. As he was standing there, admiring the young man and wondering how to get past him and into the ward, Geoff came along.

"And what are you doing here, Mike?"

Mike hesitated, and then said that he wanted to go in and see Steven.

"Mike, I know what you'd like to do to that bastard, but it's not worth it. If you went in there and if anything happened, you'd be in real shit, now go home and leave the interrogations to us."

Mike was hesitant at first, but once Geoff had explained what the consequences could be should Mike do anything to Steven, he relinquished and returned home.

Two days later, Steven was back in court and the trial was able to resume again.

Much to Mike's surprise, the defense called him to the stand to act as a character witness to Steven's behavior and mental health. Mike had told the court how Steven was disliked by most of the staff and why, and that he always passed snide, catty comments of a derogatory nature to them. None of this seemed to help the defense's case.

Pavel and Geoff were also called to the stand as the arresting officers, but nothing seemed to be going in Steven's favor. Finally, Alan was called to the witness stand. Mike was nervous for his lover, but knew that Alan had an inner strength and he'd cope with the cross-examinations.

When the defense and prosecution had finished questioning Alan, he turned to the judge and asked: "Your Honor, I know that it's not the normal thing to do in a court of law, but as it directly concerns me, I would like to know from the defendant why he shot me as opposed to someone else on the street."

"Very good point. Would the defendant care to offer a reason?"

Steven glared at Alan and Mike, but remained silent.

"I take it you do not wish to offer this gentleman an explanation?"

Steven suddenly broke down and at the top of his voice shouted at Mike and Alan:

"You make me sick. You've got everything anyone could want and I've got nothing but trouble and worry. You've got happiness together but I've got a wife that I despise and loath. I see you always laughing and joking, and it grates me to see that. You're efficient and I know that I'm not and everybody likes you at work, but they hate me, why? I shot him because I wanted you to know what it's like to suffer, know what it's like to have unhappiness in your life and possibly lose someone that you love. I know what you are," he said pointing at Mike, "and if loving a man means that much to you, I don't want to see you happy."

The court fell silent after this tirade, and then the judge spoke up.

"Mr. Bass, you sound like a very troubled man. The fact that these two men love each other is a good thing. There is too much unhappiness in this world as it is without you making it worse. I respect Mr Schwantz and his partner for their dedication to each other, especially when so much of society still discriminates against minority groups. I cannot speak for Mr Schwantz, but he seems an upright, loyal and honest young man, certainly someone I would be proud to have working for me, and that is something Mr Bass that you have not shown in this court. Mr Schwantz, I don't know who's running the gym in Mr Bass's absence, but might I suggest that you apply for his position, because I think you would make a very competent manager."

After one and a half weeks of interrogation, questioning and answering, the judge found Steven Bass a.k.a Sam Baxter guilty of murder and for dealing in drugs. It had also come out in the trial that during his time as manager of the gym, he'd been dealing in a variety of drugs and in particular, steroids to bodybuilders. For his crimes, Steven was given a life sentence, without the opportunity for parole.

With the end of the court case, it would mean the departure of Pavel and Geoff to their respective countries and the settling down of all their lives.

EPILOGUE

Mike and Alan found happiness together and are still happily living together, having grown to understand each other's desires, especially Mike's desire to dominate but also be dominated by stronger men; Alan went on to become a relatively competent journalist, and moved out of his apartment to move in permanently with Mike, although his mother is not keen on Mike's taste in decor; Brett rose in the ranks of the police force and never married Belinda, probably because he liked what he had got into with Alan and Mike, but it doesn't mean that he dislikes women – he still maintains that he's bisexual; Bruno landed a job working in the gym with Mike, and Mike became the manager and owner of the gym. As to their friendships - that never died and every year both Pavel and Geoff would come to London to take part in bodybuilding competitions and meet their buddies for a holiday and each time they would relive their sexual experiences together, and on each visit they became closer and closer power buddies.

ABOUT THE AUTHOR

Lew Bull, who lives in Johannesburg, South Africa, has been published in a number of anthologies including, among others, *Ultimate Gay Erotica 2007* and *2008, Treasure Trail, Fast Balls, Travelrotica and Travelrotica Vol. 2, Don't Ask, Don't Tie Me Up, Cruise Lines* and *My First Time Vol. 5*.

Although he is involved in education, and has a Doctorate in this field, it is writing and traveling that brings him most pleasure, and he is busy finalizing a second novel.

Made in the USA